Michelle A. Valentine Books

ISBN-13: 9781479390045

ROCK THE HEART

For questions or comments about this book, please contact the author at michellevalentineauthor@gmail.com

Rock the

Heart

(Black Falcon Series, Book One)

By Michelle A. Valentine

Dedication

To the world of metal, keep on rockin'! \m/

Chapter 1

This is the most uncomfortable seat in the entire world. The stiff leather chair nearly swallows me whole with its high back, and the bare skin on my legs stick to the seat. It's also stifling in here. If I didn't know better, I would say someone left the heat on in the middle of July. A bead of sweat trickles down my spine and I reach across the table to pour a glass of water.

I can't believe I'm this nervous. It's only a board meeting for crying out loud.

The glass meets my lips and I gulp down a drink.

My best friend of four years, Aubrey, reaches over and pats my wrist. "Sweetie, it's fine. This is no biggie."

I muster up a smile and nod. Of course it's no big deal to her. She's been through countless marketing meetings. This is my very first one. Sure, I'm only an intern, but proving myself will earn me a spot at Center Stage Marketing. Something I've wanted since my freshman year in college.

Aubrey and I both earned degrees from the University of Texas and she somehow landed an assistant position to one of the top executives in the company. They actually pay her to be here, while I'm just the annoying tag along in training.

Diana Swagger, one of the most respected female marketing executives and the president of the firm, strides in and takes her seat at the head of the long table, which fills most of the room. She's put together from head to toe—not one red hair out of place on her well groomed head. Her black suit screams money and respect, and from what I've heard about her in the staff lounge, she's a no nonsense type.

Aubrey clicks her pen next to me, ready to jot notes for her boss. Even though I'm only here to observe, I mimic her actions and do my best to pretend like I belong.

"Can anyone read the goals we discussed two weeks ago?" Diana asks while she unbuttons her jacket.

A middle-aged man, to Diana's right, rattles off a list of topics that might as well be said in a foreign language. None of the projects Center Stage currently has going are products or companies I'm familiar with, but I keep my eyes trained on him like he's the most interesting person in the world.

"…And we received the go ahead from Black Falcon's people to proceed with the children's campaign," he says.

This automatically catches my attention. Black Falcon hits a little too close to home. Most people know them for their music, but I know them because of their front man, Noel Falcon. The star-studded rocker is a huge part of my past. There isn't one childhood memory that he's not in.

Diana makes a note on her yellow, legal paper. "Good. Now we need a volunteer to go down and wine and dine Noel Falcon for a few days. We need him to know we are serious about his charity."

Everyone at the table quickly busies themselves with their paperwork in front of them. All of them avoiding Diana's stare.

Diana peers around the table. "No one is interested in this? Harold?"

The man to Diana's right looks up at her and adjusts his glasses. "Sorry, Diana. Rock stars aren't well known for working well with us boring ad types. Last time I personally tried working with one, he blew me off, then became irate that his marketing wasn't what he had envisioned. No offense, but this isn't the type of account I'm willing to take on again. It's a time suck."

Diana leans back in her chair, steeples her fingers together, and presses them to her lips. "Is no one interested?" Her eyes scan her employees one more time—all of them avoiding her stare—before they land on me. "How about you? You seem to be the only other one interested in this account."

Shit. Eye contact is a pain in the ass.

I swallow hard and my hand clutches my throat. "M—me?"

She leans forward in her seat. "I'm sure Mr. Falcon would surely give a young, pretty thing like you the time of day. All you would have to do is get him to spend some time with you and then find out exactly what his vision is for the children's charity Black Falcon is heading up."

My throat suddenly goes dry. How can I face Noel again? I want to scream at the top of my lungs I can't, but I know if I want a job at Center Stage I need to be a yes woman until I get my foot planted firmly inside this door.

I can do this—talk with an old friend on a very professional level. This might be a piece of cake.

I take another huge gulp of water, trying to calm my nerves, while Diana stares expectantly at me. If I let my history with Noel slip out she might yank this opportunity away, and I can't let that happen. Not after I'm so close to landing my dream job.

Aubrey nudges my leg under the table. She knows I'm stalling. She's heard the stories about Noel.

I set the glass down, deciding it's best to keep my relationship with him private, and nod my head. "I would love to take on this job for you."

Diana smiles and leans back in her chair. "At least someone is willing to go the distance for this company. What did you say your name was again?"

"Lanie…Lanie Vance."

Diana makes another note on the paper in front of her. "Does anyone have Black Falcon's tour schedule? We need to get Ms. Vance to their next show and get things rolling on this."

Harold types something into his tablet and quickly says, "Black Falcon's next show is tomorrow night in Houston Texas, then it appears they have a break until Rock on the Range in Columbus, Ohio a few days later."

Tomorrow? I scrunch my nose. That's a hell of a lot sooner than I expected. When I volunteered for this, I figured I would at least have a few days to mentally prepare myself. What in the hell am I going to say to Noel? Sorry for stomping on your heart four years ago? Oh and by the way I'm only here to land my dream job.

I resist the urge to bury my face in my hands. What have I just gotten myself into?

No, I have to look on the bright side. Houston is only about thirty minutes from my hometown. At least it'll be a free trip home for the weekend. It's been a couple months since I've seen my mom, and I miss her like crazy. New York is a hard place to get away from.

I can do this, right?

"Someone schedule this girl a flight for tomorrow immediately and give her the run down on this charity, so she'll know what information we need from the band," Diana says.

When I open my mouth to tell Diana I've changed my mind, Aubrey says, "Ms. Swagger, I would like to volunteer to go with Lanie. She's only an intern, and I would love to go along with her and show her the ropes on navigating clients."

Ms. Swagger nods. "Okay then, I'll allow that. Go ahead and book a flight for yourself and one for Ms. Vance and then report back to me on Monday after the initial meeting."

I slump back in the chair.

This may be the worst decision of my life.

Aubrey leads me into the hallway after the meeting is over. Every nerve in my body zings with adrenaline. This is it, my big break to show Ms. Swagger I deserve a job in her company, that I'm a marketing slave. The only problem is facing Noel.

Aubrey grabs my wrist and yanks me into the supply closet. "Oh. My. God." She shakes her head and her auburn curls bounce around her shoulders. "I don't even know what to say. On one hand, I'm thrilled you'll have the chance to show these stuffy assholes around here some of those mad marketing skills, but on the other I'm freaked the fuck out. Noel Falcon, Lanie?"

I sigh. "I know, I know, but what was I suppose to do? Tell Diana no because I have a painful history with the lead singer of Black Falcon? There's no way I could admit that to her. This opportunity just fell into my lap. I'd be crazy not to jump all over it."

Aubrey grabs my hands and squeezes them. "You're right. You can get through this. It's only Noel Falcon. We go down there and take him to dinner. You'll be fine because I'll be there the entire time for moral support."

I wrap my arms around her slender frame. "Thank you for doing this with me."

She pulls away and pushes my dark hair back before resting her hands on my shoulders. Her emerald eyes stare at me. "You're welcome, sweetie. Now there's only one thing left to do…" Her lips twist and she picks at my shirt.

I raise an eyebrow at the mischievous look on her face. "Oh, no. I know that look."

Aubrey's grin broadens. "Where's the closest mall? I can't wait to see Noel's jaw hit the floor when he sees you."

I roll my eyes and do my best to look displeased, but deep down I can't wait to see that either.

Chapter 2

The last chord of the song still hums in my ears. I can't believe I'm out here in this blistering heat. The sun beats down on my back and I just know my fair skin is going to scream at me later. But I have to be here, even if it is the last place I ever wanted to be—front row of my high school boyfriend's concert. God knows where he gets the inspiration for his music from.

The lead singer from the opening act, Embrace the Darkness, walks back on stage in his tight, black, leather pants and ripped up t-shirt. The crowd behind me is predominantly women because my old boyfriend is a rock-sex icon now. They scream even louder when the rocker grabs the microphone off the stand.

Two fights broke out behind me during the last band's set, so I'm a bit nervous to find out what's going to happen when the main act goes on, but I'm not leaving this spot. I've waited out here since the gates opened at noon to get center stage. I want the best view possible to lay my eyes on the first boy I ever really kissed.

"You guys are awesome. Thank you so much." The singer smiles and the rampant crowd of horny women shove against one another even harder to get closer to the stage. "Are you ladies ready to drop your panties for Black Falcon!?"

That gets them pumped up again. I look behind me and watch the waves of people scream and yell in excitement.

My ears ring, but I don't want to look like a total wuss and stuff my fingers in them in the midst of all these hard-core rocker chicks. That might get my ass kicked.

The middle aged woman behind me screams out Noel's name followed by an 'I love you' at least ten octaves higher than her normal voice. The woman shoves into my back, and I crunch into the iron fencing in front of me.

"Give it up for BLACK FALCON!" the rocker screams, and my insides jitter. I'm not sure why I'm nervous. It's not like he'll even remember me. He sees tons of women every night, and after a while faces probably all start to look the same to him.

My gaze instantly glues to the stage. The lead singer, Noel Falcon, enters from the right and looks just like I remember him—tall and lean with shaggy, dark-brown hair. He's not the goofy boy I knew anymore. The past four years have been good to him. Really good. He wears twenty-two well. The dark, scruffy hair on his jaw line brings out the blue in his eyes, and for a second, I kick myself for the night we broke up.

Noel stops center stage, wearing a sexy grin as he takes in the arena packed with his adoring fans. He's close. I can practically reach out and trace the intricate tattoos on his arm if I want to. The spotlight beams down on him, and he points a finger out to the throngs of people in the upper deck. The crowd goes nuts, but I stand there simply awestruck. Not because Noel Falcon, one of the hottest rockers on the planet is five feet in front of me, but because it's Noel Falcon, the first boy I ever loved. He used to be my best friend. The guy I thought at one time was my forever.

Noel pulls the microphone off the stand. "Wow!" He steps back and laughs as he stares around. He looks unbelievably hot in his jeans and tight, black t-shirt. "I can't tell you how great it feels to be back in my old stomping grounds. I grew up not far from here, so tonight—"

"I LOVE YOU NOEL!" shouts the lady behind me again, practically right in my ear.

Noel flicks his line of sight down and makes eye contact with me. Surprise registers on his face, and he pauses for a brief second, even though it feels like an eternity to me. "So tonight—" he says, still staring at me. "—is a very special night. It gives me a chance to revisit my past. See people I haven't seen since high school. The good and the bad." Noel's gaze leaves me, and he glances back out toward the crowd. "Are you guys ready to rock?"

Noel's band starts off with a fast song, and every person in the arena thrashes around. Pumping their fists and jumping around like crazy Mexican Jumping Beans.

"Oh my God, Lanie. He totally recognizes you!" Aubrey squeals in my ear while grabbing my arm.

"No he doesn't." I attempt to blow her words off. She has no clue how intense mine and Noel's relationship was back then. She's only heard stories.

"Hello? Are you kidding me? He even just said 'high school' when he looked at you. We have to put these passes to use and get back stage," Aubrey shouts as she bounces in time with the beat—her long, auburn hair trailing down her back. Tonight for her, is all about fun and the possibility of meeting one of the hottest bands around, but for me...I'm not really sure what I expect from tonight. Noel's always been the 'what if' for me. The one who got away.

Noel straps his guitar around his neck and then haphazardly slings it over his shoulder. He grabs the mic with both hands and brings it to his full lips. It reminds me of the way he used to kiss. He'd always put his entire soul into everything he did, which included the way he loved me.

"Look at me. I see you now. The way we used to be..." Noel sings in perfect rhythm.

The smoothness of his voice fills my ears, and it takes me back. I close my eyes and listen to his words and remember all the times we sat out on the old boat dock, overlooking the lake that separated our two childhood homes. That was our spot. The place we met in secret so many nights. The first place he sang to me. The first place we made love.

It was also the place where our love ended— where I told him to give up on his foolish dreams to become a rock star and do something sensible, like me, and go to college. I knew I broke his heart when I said I could never be with a dreamer because dreams don't pay the bills.

Look at what I knew.

He totally made it, while I'm still struggling to land my perfect job in this tough economy with my 'sensible' degree. Life without him, these last four years, has been lonely.

A tear rolls down my cheek. How silly was I to listen to people, that Noel was a loser going nowhere just because he loved music. We could've been happy. We could've beaten the odds. But, I guess that's something I'll never know. Just another old chapter in my life I need to walk away from because it's too late.

I open my eyes to take one last look at Noel. His eyes close as he belts out the chorus. Sweat beads illuminate his face under the spot light. He's truly beautiful. But he's a stranger now. Someone I used to know. It's time to quit torturing myself and move on. I'll just have to kiss the job at Center Stage goodbye.

"Aubrey, I need to get out of here. I can't do this," I shout to my friend.

Her pink lips twist. "Why? Because of him?" She points to Noel.

My eyes flit up to Noel's face, and at that very second, he looks down at me while he strums his guitar. His eyes hold mine for a second before I glance back at Aubrey and nod. "I have to get out of here. This is like torture."

Aubrey's whole body slumps like a deflated balloon. "You know we can't do that," she sighs. "You have to suck it up and talk to him. You won't get a job and I'll lose mine. Diana doesn't mess around." She takes my hand and pulls me through the crowd. I glance back and watch a pile of girls shove their way into our spot.

The outdoor arena is so loud I can hardly hear my own thoughts. We make it to the back of the crowd just as the song ends. People are screaming Noel's name while they're waiting for the next song to begin. When it's oddly silent, I think about taking one last look before I walk out on him again—one last look to remember him by.

"This next song goes out to the girl who shredded my heart without hesitation back in high school. It's called *Ball Busting Bitch*, and Lanie, this one's for you."

My entire body freezes and I feel my mouth go dry. What a dick! The blood in my veins boil and my fingers shake as I resist the urge to storm the stage and punch him square in the face.

On second thought that sounds like a fantastic idea.

I lunge forward and Aubrey snags my arm. "What the hell are you doing?"

"I'm going to kick his ass," I snarl.

Aubrey rolls her emerald eyes. "As much as I would love to see you do that, it's impossible and you know it. The guy probably has ten hunky bodyguards to protect him from the likes of you. Besides we have to be civil to that cretin, remember?"

My shoulders slump in defeat. Oh, right. I have a job riding on getting Noel to like me. The last thing I want to do right now is talk to him, let alone be nice to him, but what choice do I have?

"You're right. Let's just get through tonight, get the info we need, then get our asses back to New York where we belong."

Aubrey wraps her slender arm around my shoulders and gives me a little squeeze. "There's the Lanie I love. Come on. Let's weasel our way backstage and get to work."

My fingers rub over my aching forehead. This is a bad idea, but I reluctantly tell her okay. She grabs me in a tight hug—her vanilla perfume super strong in my nose—and leads me toward the restricted area sign with our backstage passes tight in hand.

Chapter 3

Being backstage at a rock show isn't as glamorous as one may think. It's filled with dirty, sweaty men—most of which are overweight and look like they haven't showered in six months. Plus, the way they leer at me is creepy, like I'm a dessert ready to be licked.

I shudder at the last thought and grip Aubrey's hand tighter.

"Damn, Lanie, loosen up. You're killin' my hand," she complains.

I drop her hand. "Sorry. Where the hell is the band? Their set has been over for at least fifteen minutes."

We come to a hallway filled with music equipment and people loitering about. Something tells me we've come to the right spot to find a rock band. The sheer volume of scantily clad women milling about shocks me. Some of them are even walking around topless like it's no big deal.

I smooth down my fitted leather halter and jean shorts, suddenly feeling like one of the only modestly dressed women around.

Do these girls have no self respect?

Aubrey runs a hand through her auburn curls. "How are we supposed to get any one on one time with him in this freak show? Harold is right, rock star accounts are definitely not the usual."

"I don't know, but we aren't leaving until we talk to him." I grab her wrist and tug her forward. "We'll check every one of these rooms if we have to."

Aubrey giggles uncontrollably as we rush from room to room throwing the red doors wide open in search of Noel Falcon. Somehow we've ended up turning this into a silly little game of shocking people as we slam open the doors. A majority of the rooms are either locked or empty, but I have the feeling if we keep this up much longer we are going to get thrown out of this place.

The last room we come to has music blasting on the other side of the red door. Aubrey twists the handle, throws open the door, and shouts, "Booyah!" at the top of her lungs, causing me to laugh so hard I double over.

"Oh, um, sorry," Aubrey says while yanking on my arm.

I stand up straight, trying to curve my giggles, and stare right into the eyes of Noel Falcon. The smile drops completely off my face.

Two topless women press against him, one on each side, and his arms wrap around them. A slow, lazy grin spreads across his face, and I suddenly feel the urge to hurl.

"Well, well, well. If it isn't my old pal, Lanie," Noel says. "Please, by all means, come in and join our little private party. I was going to take it easy tonight and settle for just these two, but you and your friend are more than welcome to join in. The more the merrier, right ladies?"

The blondes giggle and then run their hands up and down his chiseled chest while they lean in and kiss each other.

He continues smiling at me, loving that he's paying me back ten fold right now. I shake my head in disgust. "You're a real piece of shit, you know that? Come on, Aubrey."

Aubrey grabs my shoulders, holding me in place. "Lanie, we can't. What about our jobs? We have to talk to him."

I shake my head and glance at Noel. "Fuck the job. I'll pass."

I storm away from the door with Aubrey close on my heels. I don't know how I'm going to explain this to Diana Swagger, but this is just too much. It's way more than I bargained for. No sane person could speak to such a condescending, egotistical, prick of an ex-boyfriend, let alone work with him.

I'll just have to find a new dream.

Aubrey keeps up with me as I blast past all the people in the busy hallway. I'm so angry with myself. I can't believe I let myself think for a minute this would be easy or that I'm even capable of facing Noel.

The exit door flies open as I shove my way through. I gulp down the thick, Texas night air and push my hair back from my face. I'm not even sure how to find our rental car from this area of the parking lot, but I keep trudging forward. I need distance as much as I can from Noel Falcon.

"Damn, Lanie, would you wait up? These boots aren't exactly made for running a marathon," Aubrey complains behind me.

I sigh and stop in my tracks. "Aubrey, you just don't—"

"What?" her tone snaps. "Don't understand? If you tell me that one more time after I've listened to you pine after him for four freakin' years, then I'm going to murder you here and now. Capiche? I know what he meant to you and how much tonight hurt you, but now you know there isn't anything left for you there. You can move on. Forget about Noel Falcon and focus on your career. That douche is the only thing standing between you and your dream job, go back in there and face him. Get your answers."

She's right. I can't let my emotions come get in the way of the biggest career opportunity I'll ever have. "Alright. Jeesh. You don't have to go and get all mafia on me. I'll think about it."

Aubrey tilts her head and pops her bottom lip out. "Please, Lanie. Please? I need you as my coworker."

My fingers rub over my aching forehead. She's not going to let this go, is she? Even though I know this is a bad idea, I reluctantly tell her okay. She squeaks and grabs me up into a tight hug.

She pulls back. "You're doing the right thing."

I frown. Second thoughts plague me, and my gut twists into a knot. Maybe this isn't such a good idea after all.

When we return to the building, it seems even more crowded than before as we find ourselves weaving between people, like we're in a packed night club. The red doors in the hallway remain shut, and I cringe when I think about what's behind the last one.

Aubrey stops me. "Sure you don't want to wait for him to come out? I can only imagine what's going on in there now."

I shake my head. "No. If I wait, I'll lose my nerve. We are getting what we came for. Do me a favor, though?"

"Anything."

"When I toss the two hookerbots out, keep them out. I can't fight both of them and get info from Noel at the same time."

I turn and shove open the door and storm through. "Alright everyone get the—"

Noel glances up from his guitar and glares at me. "Can I help you?"

I shut the door, closing the two of us alone in the small room. "Where'd your sluts go?"

Noel's eyes narrow. "Why? You jealous or...maybe, they're more your type now."

"Fuck you." It slips out before I remember I need to stay calm here.

He laughs and then strums his guitar. "No thanks. For some reason, I'm not in the mood anymore."

I sigh and run my fingers through my hair. "Look, Noel. I didn't come here to fight with you."

Noel raises a pierced eyebrow. "Really? Tell me then, Lane, why *did* you come here?"

'Lane.' It's been so long since I've heard that. Noel is the only person alive who shortens my name.

I shake the memories away. This isn't a time to reminisce. It's time to get down to business. "Well…" I clear my throat. "I'm an intern at Center Stage Marketing, and my boss, Diana Swagger, flew me down here to discuss Black Falcon's charity with you."

"You?" He shakes his head. "Out of all the people in the entire fucking world, they send you down here to talk to me. Did they think because we've fucked before I wouldn't fire you?"

My hands ball into fists at my side. "How can you say that to me? I'm not one of your groupie whores, Noel. What we had was real!"

He lays his guitar down and stands in front of me—his six foot two frame towers over me. "Then why did you leave me, huh? Tell me that. If it was so real, why did you walk away from it?"

I can't look at him. The reasons for me leaving him that night, on the dock, are unbelievably selfish. Noel reaches out and takes a strand of my brown hair between his fingers and twirls it just like he always did when we were a couple.

I slap his hand away. His touch is just too soon.

The corners of his lips turn down. He reaches back up and tucks the loose strand of my hair behind my ear. His fingertips linger on my cheek. "Why do you always fight against the inevitable? You've always made things so difficult."

I take a step away from him, but he closes the gap between us even tighter—his chest against mine. "There is no inevitable with us, Noel."

"Sure there is. Fate brought you here, didn't it?" Noel cradles my face in both hands. I try to pull away, but he doesn't let me go. A smile flirts along his lips. "You look exactly the same. Still the most beautiful girl I've ever seen." He brings his lips toward mine. Warmth from his breath touches my face and all I can think about is kissing him. What it would feel like. Would it be just like old times? "How about a kiss? Don't you remember how hot things were between us?"

My heart thunders with anticipation, and I bite my bottom lip. He runs his nose along my jaw line and I close my eyes and inhale his spicy sent. He smells delicious. Noel's eyes search my face while his lips hover over mine.

I can feel the heat of him against my face and my legs tremble.

He leans in closer but stops just short of my lips and whispers, "Now you know what it's like to want something you can't have."

His hands drop away from my face. There's no emotion on his face, but his eyes look pained and it crushes me to know I have this effect on him.

Noel steps back and runs his hand through his shaggy hair before stepping around me and walking out the door.

The breath, I didn't even realize I'm holding, expels from my chest when the door closes. I feel like I should say something, maybe even apologize for what I did to him four years ago, but I can't. The ground holds my feet steady as I hear the door open behind me. My heart falls around my ankles, and I think about how easy it's going to be for him to stomp on it while it's down. I know I don't deserve any kindness from him, but the blatant smack in the face of emotion still hurts like hell. This is my payback from Noel—to hurt.

A small pair of hands rest on my shoulders. "Did you get your answers?"

I nod, but can't bring myself to turn and face Aubrey. "Everything I needed to know."

Chapter 4

This is the first time since the start of my internship a month ago, that I hate being at work. It's going to be hard to admit I failed. Noel didn't tell me jack crap about his charity. The only information I have about it, is that it's some type of children's charity.

I pinch the bridge of my nose. He knows what the job meant to me. He took this away from me on purpose, and it pisses me off.

Aubrey leads us into the conference room for our scheduled meeting with Diana and the rest of the executive staff at Center Stage. My stomach rolls as I take a seat and scoot closer to the table. I fold my hands on top of the notepad I brought with me and take a deep breath.

Ms. Swagger takes her seat, and looks at me before slipping on her glasses. "Ms. Vance, would you care to fill us in on how your meeting with Mr. Falcon went?"

The finger nails of my left hand dig into the skin on the back of the opposite hand. Telling this woman I screwed up will be like nailing my own coffin shut, but what other choice do I have?

I readjust myself in the chair. "Actually, Ms. Swagger, I—"

She holds up a finger toward me, asking for me to pause, before she pushes a button on the intercom in front of her. "Jillian, dear, there isn't any water in the conference room. Could you see that some is brought in immediately?"

"Right away, Ms. Swagger," the secretary replies. I can tell by the response Diana always gets what she wants.

Without skipping a beat, Diana turns her attention back to me. "Ms. Vance, can I just say I've never received a phone call quite like the one I got from Mr. Falcon yesterday."

My heart leaps into my throat. Oh God. Here comes the boot. I need to do every thing I can to keep my internship. "I can explain about that."

Diana leans back in her chair. "Please do. It seems some of my account executives could learn a thing or two about reeling in a client."

My brow furrows, and I glance over at Aubrey who just shrugs in response. "I'm sorry, but I'm a little confused. What exactly did Noel—er, Mr. Falcon say?"

"We had a lengthy conversation about the long term goals of the marketing campaign for his children's literacy program, and Mr. Falcon is adamant that you take the lead on this project. He seems to think you are the only person on my team that understands him and his goals. Of course, I explained that you were only an intern and that I felt it best for someone with more experience head this up, but Mr. Falcon blatantly refused. He said he wants you, and you only, or he pulls the account from us."

My eyes widen. "Are you offering me a job?"

Diana smiles and removes her glasses. "Yes, with the stipulation that you are successful with the Black Falcon project. If it fails, then I'll have no choice but to let you go."

All the eyes of the other marketing team members focus on my reaction. Children's literacy hits home for Noel. He grew up with dyslexia and reading was always a struggle for him and he knows that I know that about him. It explains why he thinks I'm the best person for his job.

I rub the back of my neck as I feel the weight of the pressure push down. Even though I've known him forever, I don't understand why on earth Noel would make that kind of request? He hates me now. He made that perfectly clear back in Houston. Why would he want me around more—to torture me, probably.

Is a job really worth all of this?

I have to grab this opportunity with both hands and do my best to keep my relationship with Noel strictly professional.

I swallow hard. Those are some hefty stakes, but I'm willing to take it on. "Understood."

She nods. "Good. Welcome to the Center Stage family. Aubrey, see that Human Resources changes Ms. Vance's employment status to full-time."

I watch my best friend make a note in her elegant script. "Yes, Ms. Swagger."

"Oh, and Aubrey, find this young lady a desk so she can get to work." Diana winks at me before moving on to the next order of business.

After the meeting ends and everyone clears out of the room, Aubrey yanks me into a tight hug. "Oh my God, Lanie. What the hell just happened? Instead of getting the boot, you get handed a job on a platter. I thought you said Noel didn't tell you anything."

My head spins. All this doesn't seem real. "He didn't. When we were in Texas, it was like he couldn't get away from me fast enough."

She twists her ruby, red lips into a slight grin. "Sounds like he's doing whatever he can to keep you close."

I roll my eyes. "He only wants to punish me for breaking up with him. You saw how he loved shoving the two naked skanks in my face."

Aubrey sighs. "That was pretty gross, I'll give you that, but it wasn't like he meant to do that, Lanie. He didn't know that we'd come busting through the door unannounced."

"Yes, he did. He even invited us to join. Ugh," I growl in frustration. "Whose side are you on, anyway?"

"Yours, always yours, you know that. All I'm saying is he did go out of his way to make sure you got this job. Would he really do that just to get back at you? Give him a chance. Maybe it was an off night. He might actually want to be friends again."

I shrug. Damn her. Why does she have to be so rational?

Aubrey smiles, "When you meet up with him again, plaster on the biggest smile you can muster and win him over. He's the key to keeping your job. Remember the old saying, 'fake it 'til you make it'?"

I nod. That's exactly what I have to do "You're right. I'll do whatever it takes to keep this job."

"Of course I am. Now, let's go pick out your future shitty cubical." Aubrey giggles and pulls me into the hallway.

An hour later, I sit at my new desk staring at Noel's contact information on the computer screen. What am I going to say to him? I mean, do I thank him for basically getting me this job or do I play it cool and pretend his phone call didn't pull any strings. Either way, I have to call him. Talking with Noel is the only way I can get things rolling. The only thing I know about the charity he's trying to establish is, it's for children's literacy.

I rub my forehead vigorously. It's just a stupid phone call. How hard can it be?

The nerves in my hand twitch when I pick up the phone. Each number punch makes my stomach knot a little tighter and when it rings my skin grows cold and clammy.

Noel answers on the fourth ring. "Yeah?"

I tuck my hair behind my ear. "Noel? Hi. It's Lanie Vance and I'm—"

He chuckles. "Lane Vance, to what do I owe this pleasure?"

I squeeze the phone tighter in my hand. "Actually, I was calling on behalf of Center Stage Marketing. I've been assigned to your account and I wanted to touch base with you."

"Touch base?" He laughs. "Listen to you sounding all professional. If you really want to touch my base, that can be arranged. All you have to do is ask."

The nerve of this guy is unbelievable. "Ugh. You're a real asshole, you know that?"

"Yes, as a matter of fact, I do know that. Thanks to you. You made that quite clear last time I saw you."

Play nice, Lanie. Remember?

This is harder than I thought. The sweet, sensitive guy I knew once is long gone. This guy is self-centered and egotistical. It's taking every inch of my self control not to tell him to shove this job right up his leather covered ass.

I take a deep breath and remember what Aubrey said about smiling. "You're right, and I'm...I'm sorry about that. I was out of line, even just a moment ago. There's no reason two old friends can't get along and work together on a project."

Noel's silent for a moment and then he says, "Friend, huh? Ouch."

I shake my head. There's no way we are going down that old road. "You know what I mean."

"You're right, Lane. We should be friends, but there's only one problem with that scenario."

"And what would that be?" I bite my lip, hating the fact that I'm thinking of how sexy he probably looks right now. I picture him spread out on a bed, shirtless, still exhausted from the night before.

"I can't be friends with someone who hates me." The sexy vision of him bursts and I'm thrown back into reality.

"Noel...I never said I hated you."

"You didn't have to. I saw it all over your face," he says with a sharp tone.

"That wasn't hate, Noel."

"Then what was it?"

"Disgust," I say instantly. "Don't you have any self-respect? You just sleep with any slut that throws herself your way? That's not the Noel I know."

"It's not like that," he growls, frustrated into the phone. "Forget it. I don't have to explain anything to you."

"You know what? You're right. You don't owe me any explanations. Who you sleep with is none of my business. However, *my* business with you is now professional and I really need some details about this charity. My job is riding on how well it turns out, so you've got to give me something."

"So you got the job?" He sounds surprised and even a little excited.

I debate on which tactic to use, but I decide to play it straight with him. Noel's not stupid. "Yes, actually, thanks to you. That phone call you made to Diana Swagger made it possible."

"Good." I can hear a smile in his voice. "It's the least I could do after blowing you off the way I did."

"Well, thank you for that. This job means a lot to me."

"I know it does. That's why I felt like a total tool and had to make it right."

I chew on the inside of my jaw. It is kind of sweet that he cared enough about my feelings to make that phone call. Maybe he's not the complete dirtball I thought. This might work. A small glimmer of hope shines in my heart for a split second that we may be able to overcome our past and keep things civil.

"So...Noel, about this charity"—I clear my throat— "what is your vision for the project?"

Noel yawns into the phone, and my feathers ruffle. I'm boring all of the sudden? Two minutes ago we were fighting. I shake my head. I'll never get a good read on this guy with his crazy up and down signals.

"Lane, these business calls tend to put me asleep. I'd much rather see you in person to discuss all of this. Maybe you can wear something skimpy to keep me focused on you and what you're saying."

I roll my eyes. "Whatever, Noel." Before I let the severely rude things on my mind fly from my mouth I take a deep breath and remind myself, yet again, that I need to get him to like me. I soften my voice and say, "That's kind of impossible. It's not like you're here, right around the corner in New York."

"Actually, I *am* in New York."

My heart does a double thump against my ribs. "You—you are?"

"Yep. Did some press last night for our next album, and I decided to stay a couple nights and check out the local scene. So, what do you say to dinner with me tonight?"

This is a curve ball I'm not prepared to catch.

"I don't think a date is a very good idea. You're technically my client now and that wouldn't be very professional."

"Don't think of it as a date. Think of it more as a business meeting."

I look down at the notepad in front of me, and my hand freezes. Seven doodle hearts stare back at me. Is my subconscious trying to tell me something? I hope not.

"A business dinner would be fine." What's the harm in meeting him for job related purposes?

"Great. Give me your cell, and I'll text you the time and place."

We say our goodbyes after I give him my cell phone number. *Dinner with Noel Falcon?* It's been a long time since I've said that, and I'm wondering if it's a good idea to trudge down old paths. I only hope I can keep my head on straight and maintain a business relationship with him. God knows if he touches me the way he did in Houston, he'll be pretty fucking hard to resist.

Chapter 5

The cab stops at the corner of 57th street, near the restaurant where I'm suppose to meet Noel. I pay the driver and give him a scathing look as he lifts his butt out of his seat to get a better look down the top of my dress in the review mirror.

Men? Are they all such scumbags?

Nu Boo restaurant is one of the hottest places in the city to dine, which makes it very hard to get a reservation without advance notice. Noel obviously managed to obtain one last minute, but somehow I'm not surprised. He is Noel Falcon, and whether I want to admit it or not, he has magical connections.

This restaurant is a prime example of that.

I step up to the hostess and feel my face flush when she asks for the name my reservation is under. "I'm actually meeting the other member of my party here. The name is under…" I hesitate and think about how absurd the pseudo name Noel gave is. "Um, it's under Dong, Long-Dick Dong."

The young, blonde waitress snickers, and the flesh around my ears burn. There's no doubt that my complexion is the same color as the slinky red dress Aubrey insisted I wear tonight.

The girl gains her composure, and says, "Right this way, Ms. Dong."

I want to crawl in a hole and die from sheer embarrassment.

I spot Noel in a corner table talking on his cell. His laugh cuts through the dinner crowd chatter and my stomach knots. He still laughs the same and it takes me back to the time when we were in love. It's only been four years. Memories of us together are still vivid and I picture his face. I bite my lip as I shake away the thought. Hopefully, I can maintain a line between our business and personal relationship.

A hulking man steps in front of me and the hostess. He's at least six foot five with a short buzz cut and bulging forearms. He looks like he can kill someone with his bare hands. "I'm sorry, ladies. Mr. Falcon isn't available for pictures or autographs at this time."

The hostess shrugs and turns to me. "You're on your own from here. Good luck."

I swallow hard and stare up at the big guy who's blocking my path to Noel. "I'm Lanie Vance?" It sounds more like a question than a statement when the words leave my mouth. "He's expecting me."

The bodyguard's eyes soften. The menacing look he wore a second ago gone as he stands aside. "My apologies, Ms. Vance, please proceed."

I tell him thank you, then step around him. Noel glances up and notices me. His jaw drops a little as his hungry eyes rake over my body. The surprise leaves his face, and a slow, sexy grin spreads across his devilishly-kissable lips.

He lays his phone on the table without telling the other person goodbye as he stands to greet me. Even in a simple outfit of a white button-up shirt and jeans, Noel looks delicious. The sleeves of his white shirt are shoved up to his elbows, revealing tattoos covering every inch of his impressive forearms. The disheveled sweaty hair I'd last seen him in, now styled into a trendy fohawk and his chin sporting a trim goatee.

Damn. Why did he have to be so sexy? A girl can only resist so much when someone looks the way he does.

"Wow." He kisses my cheek and hugs me a little too tightly against his chest for a business greeting. He smells divine, like a body wash and something else entirely male. He trails his nose along my cheek and then whispers in my ear, "You look good enough to eat."

I pull away and place a hand on his chest to push him back until his drops his arms from around my waist. "Noel, you can't say things like that to me."

He tilts his head and studies me. "Why not? It's true."

My eyes flit down to his mouth and stare at the way his lips move when he speaks. They are mesmerizing, and it takes me a second to remember why I'm here. "Just because, you can't. Not anymore, okay? This is my job."

I slide into my chair at the table, and Noel pushes my chair in for me before taking the seat directly across from me at the tiny round table. He grins at me. "So no innocent flirting?"

I shake my head. "None."

He rests his chin in the palm of his hand and stares at me openly with his big, blue eyes. "Is it because you have a boyfriend?"

I scrunch my eyebrows together. "What? Who said anything about me having a boyfriend?"

Thoughts of my last boyfriend, Corey, shoot through my mind. That relationship ended over two years ago, and since then, I've found school and work more fulfilling than dating college boys with one night stands on the brain.

He smiles. "If there's no boyfriend in the picture, I don't see why I can't compliment you for looking down right sexy."

I rub across the back of my neck and toy with my hair. It shouldn't matter that he thinks I'm sexy, but it does. Heat in my belly pools, and I fight the urge to reach out and trail my fingers over his skin.

I can't let him do this. Noel cannot take control over this situation. I need him to like me, but also keep him at a distance. We aren't crazy, reckless teenagers anymore. The sweet talk that won me over in high school can't go on now. We're adults and we need to act like it.

I readjust in my chair and cross my legs under the table. "Well, thank you for the compliment, but I would appreciate that in the future we keep our relationship strictly professional. I have a lot riding on you and me getting along, so I would like you to refrain from those types of compliments."

I cringe inwardly as I wait for Noel to tell me to get the hell out of the restaurant. I'm sure he's used to getting his way now days. Isn't that how all the tabloids portray rock stars? Putting him in his place probably isn't going to sit well. After all, I don't really deserve any kindness from him after the way I broke up with him, so he has every right to be angry with me.

However, instead of harsh words, I hear Noel roar with laughter across from me.

A few heads at surrounding tables turn toward us. Does this man attract attention everywhere he goes?

I smooth the white linen table cloth with my finger and try to pretend that his laugh isn't kind of insulting. He finds it funny that I asked him to not sexually pursue me?

He wipes a tear away from his eye. "Lane, I never knew you had this little hard-ass business chick inside of you. I have to admit, this no-nonsense attitude is kind of hot. Plus, I didn't know you thought about riding me. That's one thing I know I can make happen for you."

Great. So not the reaction I want. He's never going to take me seriously. I'm a fool for thinking I could make this work out.

I grab my purse and start to stand.

Noel reaches across the table and grabs my wrist. His blue eyes ablaze. "Wait, where are you going, Lane? We haven't even ordered dinner yet."

His fingers burn my skin, and I stare up at the ceiling and count to three to take my mind off how good his touch feels. I pull my arm away from his grasp. "Professional, please, Noel."

He raises his hands in surrender. "Okay, if I promise to keep things PG, will you stay?"

Does he even know how to do that anymore? This whole cocky, rock star persona he's got going on probably warps his rating system of what's actually considered PG.

I tuck my hair behind my ear and sigh. "PG? If you can do that, I'll stay."

Noel crosses his finger over his heart. "I'll be on my best behavior."

I raise an eyebrow and pick up a menu. "That's what I'm afraid of."

Noel chuckles. "I don't remember you being this fun back in high school."

"Yeah, well, I don't remember you being this much of a dick." I duck behind the menu and bit the inside of my cheek and curse myself for talking to him this way. I'm going to lose this job before dinner is even over.

He clears his throat. "You know, Lane. If you keep talking to me like that, I might have to show you just how *nice* I can be."

"Um, that's not happening," I flip the page in the menu and do the best I can to ignore his outrageous flirting. PG doesn't seem to be in Noel's DNA.

"You say that now, but I remember how much you liked it."

My throat tightens and my thigh muscles tense. He's right. Sex with Noel was amazing, but that's not something I'm going to let happen, clearly since that seems to be his sole purpose in reuniting with me.

Uncomfortable as to where this conversation may lead, I search for a quick out. "Excuse me, Miss?" I say to a waitress that's passing by and I'm relieved when she stops at our table and cuts Noel off. "We're ready to order." The cute blonde stands with her hands behind her back, committing our orders to memory, but before she leaves I add, "I'm kind of in a rush, so the sooner you can bring our order the better."

The quicker I can get away from Noel, the sooner I'll be able to regain my sanity is what I really want to say to her, but I don't want Noel to know he's having any effect on me.

When we're alone and there's no menu to hide behind, I stare at Noel. His eyes watch me intently, studying my every move, and he makes no move to pretend that he's not openly staring at me.

I tuck a strand of my hair behind my ear. It's hard to get comfortable under his gaze. "What?"

Noel shrugs. "Just wondering what's more important than your job?"

My eyes widen. "Nothing is more important than this job."

He nods. "Good, I'm glad to hear that because it's about to take up every minute of your life."

"What do you mean?" I expect my new position will take up most of my time, but every minute?

Noel leans forward on his elbows. "I need to make sure the person in charge of getting the word out about my charity gets it—how close I am to literacy. So I've decided you have to come on the road with me to fully understand what I need from you."

Go on the road with him? Is he insane? That's unheard of, and it's totally unreasonable to ask that of me. "You can't be serious."

"Why wouldn't I be serious about this? I want to make sure you don't fuck up my charity with your lack of experience. This means a lot to me."

"I know it does, but just because I'm not all that experienced doesn't mean I won't do a great job for you, Noel. Dyslexia isn't something to be ashamed of. Lots of people have it now-a-days. You should let other people know that you have it. It may inspire some kids not to give up. But making me go on the road with you because you think I'm the only person who will understand why this literacy program means so much to you, it's...absurd."

He flinches. "Absurd? You know what's absurd? Calling the owner of a marketing company and demanding she give you a job, even though you aren't qualified because I feel like an asshole. The least you can do is come on the road with me so I can personally oversee this project and make sure I'll be happy with the finished campaign."

"I'm sorry, Noel. I didn't mean any disrespect, but you can't expect me to leave my life and ride on a cramped bus with you and a bunch of sweaty guys."

"Technically, there's only four of us on the bus, so I don't think that qualifies as 'a bunch', besides I was hoping you'd spend most of your nights with me in my room"—I raise my eyebrows and he smiles—"working on the project. The bus is the only place we'll be able to meet without interruption."

I shake my head. "I can't. Besides, Mrs. Swagger will never agree to that."

Noel traces his lower lip with his index finger and then winks at me. "You leave her to me. That old broad loves me."

"Even if I protest?"

He shrugs. "It's up to you whether you come with me or not. Guess we'll see how much you want this job."

"This is blackmail!" I seethe.

"No, see that's where you are wrong. If it were blackmail, I would get something I want out of the deal, and from what I can tell, that's not going to be an option with you. Come on, Lane. I'm not asking you to fuck me, unless you want to, that is. All I'm trying to do is help an old friend out and make sure my shit gets done right."

When he puts it that way, I do feel like an uppity jerk. Noel did get me this job. Is it really so far fetched that he wants to make sure I do a good job? I'm sure Diana told him I have zero real world experience because she told me herself she tried to talk him out of using me for the position.

But the Noel I know looks at all the angles, and I'm curious as to what his ultimate goal in this situation is. "I'm calling bullshit, Noel. Tell me, exactly what you hope to get by dragging me along on your bus?"

His lips quirk and I know I'm right. "I forgot how well you know me, Lane. You're right. There is something I hope to accomplish with this little venture."

I raise my eyebrow, curious as to what he'll say next. "And what's that?" Judging by the sexy twinkle in his eye, I have the uneasy feeling I already know.

My hand trembles as I sip my water, ruining the unfazed-by-you-Noel-Falcon look, I'm trying my best to project.

He leans across the small dinning table. His nearness causes a chemical reaction inside of me and I'm suddenly hot all over. I take another sip of water just as he says, "The chance to get back inside that tight, little body of yours."

I nearly spit the contents of my drink in his face. "Are you out of your fucking mind? How dare you say something like that to me?"

Noel's smile widens. "Because you and I both know this is going to happen. It's only a matter of time before you give into me. It isn't like I don't already know every inch of your body and what it likes. You want it just as much as I do. I can see it in your eyes."

Heat burns between my legs, and I squirm in my seat. I hate that he's having this effect on me. If I lose the upper hand in this situation, I could lose more than my job. I have to keep control here. I shake my head and try to keep images of his naked body and what it might feel like with him deep inside me out of my mind. "No. Been there, done that, not happening again."

He leans back in his chair with a smug look on his face. "We'll see."

get me a nice cushy job, but I can't string him along forever. Noel's not going to willingly hand over Black Falcon's publicity campaign over to me, without something in return, and that something he wants, he isn't getting from me. I have no intentions of sleeping with a man who is a total womanizer.

All he wants is to get back into my panties. Sex with him is probably amazing now, but a one-night stand is not worth the risk of my career...or my heart.

But I want to do this on my own merit. Diana will have no choice but to promote me once I prove I can sell anything to the masses and get Noel's account under my belt.

I rub the back of my neck. "With all due respect, Ms. Swagger, I'm not sure he's willing to give us the entire account."

Diana leans forward and taps her desk. "That's where you're wrong, Lanie. You see, I'm a shrewd business woman. I didn't get where I am by playing fair. Noel Falcon wants you on tour with him, and only you, at the expense of my company. He made that quite clear. So I agreed to send you, but gave him a condition of my own. At the end of his tour in two weeks, he has to hand over every possible marketing avenue of Black Falcon to us."

This sounds an awful lot like a trade and it makes me shiver. Is Diana actually telling me, she sold me to Noel for exclusive rights to Black Falcon? This can't be legal. I should say no. I should tell her to go to hell and walk away from the whole damn situation, but my feet won't budge.

I can do this. "Only two weeks, correct?"

Ms. Swagger nods. "Yes, only two. That'll fly by. All you have to do is keep Mr. Falcon happy and your job here is permanent."

Where else will this type of opportunity fall into my lap? I'm only twenty-two years old. Most people won't have their own accounts until they've been out of college a few years. If I say no, I'll throw away my dream.

I square my shoulders. "I'll do it."

Diana smiles, and instead of it being friendly, it seems slightly evil. My muscles tense and I lean away from her. I don't like the way she's grinning at me, and the instinct to run like hell fills my entire being.

****

My cell chirps on the coffee table as Aubrey walks into the room. She rolls her eyes and smiles. "Mr.

Wonderful, again? You still owe me some juicy details about your dinner date, you know."

I roll my eyes at her. "A lady never kisses and tells. Besides you already know nothing happened. It was strictly business."

Aubrey laughs and plops down on the couch beside me. "You, missy, are no lady. So, dish."

I shake my head. "Nothing happened the other night. I swear."

She folds her legs under herself and takes a huge bite of her double-brownie ice cream. "Bull. You expect me to believe Noel Falcon makes a romantic date with you and after a couple of hours together nothing happens? He's texted you at least fifty times over the past few days, and there was no sex involved? I say bull. No man gets that sprung unless he gets a little somethin'-somethin' if you know what I mean."

I shrug. "Getting romantic with Noel is the last thing on my mind." But getting naked and sweaty is the first. The aggressive nature he's pursuing me with, pushes every hotness button in my psyche. It's hard not to think about that when someone who looks that good continually talks about getting into my pants. But there's no need to go into detail about how much I crave the caress of his fingers on my skin with Aubrey. My sexual fantasies aren't really anyone's business.

She eyes me and licks her spoon. "So he's PG-13, huh? That's kind of disappointing. Not much of a 'Sex-god' is he? I figured as much as you talked about him he'd have you out of your panties within the hour."

"Aubrey!" I smack her leg. "I can't believe you just called him that."

"What? A 'Sex-god'?" She says around her spoon. "I got the name from you. That's how you always referred to him, but I'm thinkin' of revoking his title after the boring business date story you just told me."

It's true, I kept tabs on Noel while he shot up through the ranks of stardom. The internet is a wonderful tool for discreetly checking up on people. There are always pictures of him at parties surrounded by small mobs of women—some even famous starlets who are notorious for having flings with rock stars. Noel's been referred to as a 'Sex-god' by more than one article.

"Well, there are other single guys in the band…" That gives me an idea. "Why don't you meet us at a show or something?"

"Are you serious?" I can hear the excitement in her voice.

"Totally serious. I know how much you wanted to get back stage and meet the guys before, so I figure I kind of owe you."

I get my laptop from my bag and pull up Black Falcon's tour schedule. We pick the next Texas tour date on the schedule, so Aubrey can see her folks plus visit me and the band on the road.

My phone chirps again, and I snatch it off the table. It makes me jump when it rings in my hand.

I click the green button and say, "Why, if it isn't my favorite stalker."

Noel laughs into the phone, and I wish it didn't make me smile. "That's right, baby. You're looking really sexy in that black lingerie while lying on your bed. I'm so glad I have the perfect spot to see into your bedroom window from this tree."

I glance down at the over-sized t-shirt and socks I'm wearing. "You'd be sadly disappointed if you actually saw what I wear to bed."

"You know, clothes are overrated as far as I'm concerned. I'm good with you totally doing away with them when you visit me." I can hear the smile in his voice.

"Noel..." I say his name like a warning.

Aubrey looks over at me and rolls her eyes. "I'm going to bed," she whispers. "We can watch this movie some other time."

"Goodnight," I tell her before she closes herself in her bedroom.

"Telling your boyfriend goodnight, are ya?" Noel asks, his voice tight.

My heart pauses and then restarts within a second. I grab the pillow from the couch and hug it tight against my body. "What boyfriend?"

A loud moan of a woman in the throws of passion sounds in the background. Is he actually watching porn while he's talking to me? There's a rustling noise on Noel's end of the line and then the sound of a door closing.

"Noel?" I ask, afraid I've lost him.

"Sorry," he says, "I had to close the door. This tour bus gets crazy after a show. I can barely hear you."

I shake the images of topless groupies out of my head. "Yeah. Sorry. What were you saying?"

He tsks playfully. "I was asking you about your boyfriend. It's cool if you don't want to tell me about him."

I laugh. He's being ridiculous and reminds me a little of his old self. "You know I don't have a boyfriend."

"Good thing. I'd hate to have to hop a plane at this time of night just to kick his ass for messing around with my girl."

I smile and chew on my bottom lip. His forwardness is kind of cute. I'll give him that. "I'm not your girl, Noel."

"Not yet, but soon," he says. His confidence is disgusting. "You know I haven't even thought about sleeping with another girl since the other night."

I grin and poke fun at his comment. "Me either."

He chuckles. "I'm so glad you haven't thought about being with any other girls. Chicks would be stiff competition for me. Although, I won't say I wouldn't like to watch that."

I shake my head. Same old Noel—always a jokester. This little innocent flirting game he wants to play seems fairly harmless and if it keeps me in his good graces, then I'll play along. "You know what I meant. Besides, you're the only *stiff* competition I like."

He groans into the phone. "That's it. Where's my private jet? The word stiff coming out of your mouth is enough to send me over the edge here."

We are both quiet for a couple seconds. Jokes aside, I know he's trying to be serious. He's trying to test me. The line between our new business relationship and our old love life isn't clearly defined. It's not entirely his fault, either. I find myself looking forward to his calls and texts. Shouldn't I be dreading them?

He sighs into the phone. "Have you packed?"

I glance at my bedroom and think about the half full suitcase on my bed. "Nearly finished."

"Lane," he says, hesitation in his voice. "I know you're having second thoughts about this, but I told you, you won't be my direct employee. You work for a real marketing firm—a huge one. This looks great on your resume. Let me help you put that hard earned marketing degree to use. Everyone who gets these kinds of jobs knows someone to get their foot in the door."

Deep down, I know Noel is right. Center Stage Marketing is one of the largest firms in New York. His offer, to be in charge of promoting his children's literacy charity is amazing. The only problem is the tour. I'm stuck with him everyday. But, honestly can't think of a way around it. He made it clear if I want this job, this is the stipulation. "I'll be ready."

"Yeah?" I don't even need to see his face to know he's smiling. "That didn't take as much convincing as I thought it would."

"Well, you know, I would still be an intern if it weren't for you. I would like to be able to pay my own rent for a change. Begging my mom to cover it while I intern majorly sucks. But, if it weren't for her, Aubrey would've kicked me out of this place two years ago."

"Having money is nice," he agrees. "I remember all too well what being a starving artist is like."

"Please, your parents would never let you starve."

He's quiet. I expect at any moment he'll crack some joke like he always does, but it doesn't happen. Did I step on a touchy subject? "Noel?"

He sighs into the phone. "Yeah, I'm here."

He's frowning. I can tell by the tone in his voice. I panic. "I'm sorry if I—"

"Don't worry about it, Lane. I guess I should have told you that Dad and I really don't talk any more. For some reason, I figured you already knew that, seeing as how our families are still neighbors and all."

I hadn't had the nerve to face his parents since our break-up. They still live beside my Mom on Cedar Creek Lake in Texas. The only time I've had any contact with them is at my father's funeral three years ago, but I wasn't up for much talking having just lost my father to cancer. There's so much that has changed in our lives.

"I didn't know, Noel. I'm sorry if I upset you. You want to talk about it?"

The line is silent for a long time, but I can hear slow and steady breaths on the other end. I don't understand it. What could be so bad that Noel wouldn't speak to his father? Doesn't he know that family can be stripped away at any moment? I know his father. He's stern. The kind of man who always gets his way and people don't cross. Those two always butted heads when we were kids, especially, when it came to Noel's grades. His father couldn't grasp why school was such a struggle for his dyslexic son.

Noel's mother, on the other hand, is a lovely woman, and she's always considerate of Noel's learning disability. I can't even count the number of different tutors she hired to help him.

Noel is a mixture of both of them, I guess. His sweetness comes from his mom, while his need for complete control comes from his father. But, since I've reconnected with him, seems like his father's genes are winning out. He's pushy, just like him.

The relationship with his father was always strained when we were young. The constant need for perfection and success wore on Noel a lot. He always tried to please his father, but something in the last four years has changed, and I'm dying to find out what.

"Noel, I mean it, we've been friends a long time. You can tell me."

He lets loose a loud, shaky sigh. "It's nothing. Forget I even brought it up."

I press the pillow tighter against my chest and for some reason I wish it's Noel. The need to wrap my arms around him and tell him things will work out grips my heart. I know better than to believe that this isn't a big deal. Not being able to see his family, when they meant so much to him, must be crushing.

He should talk about this with someone. If he won't tell me willingly, I'm going to have to force it out of him.

"Bullshit," I say.

"Excuse me?" He questions with a sharp tone.

"You heard me, Noel. Bull…shit. This isn't *nothing*. Tell me. I'm your oldest friend, and I want to know what happened that's so terrible you don't see your parents anymore."

Another heavy breath on the line—he's wavering. Noel knows how relentless I can be. "He gave me an ultimatum. Go to college or get cut off."

My eyes widened. "He threw you out? Your mom let that happen?"

Noel sighs. "She tried to stop him, but Dad was hell bent on teaching me a lesson. The only thing he let me leave with was my car. Good thing that old Chevelle has a huge back seat. It was my home for quite a while."

"I'm so sorry, Noel. Why didn't you call me? I would've let you come and stay with me at the dorm." The thought of me dumping him coupled with what happened with his father causes an ache in my soul. He didn't deserve to be tossed aside like he didn't matter.

"I was too proud. I wanted to prove to you and my dad that I could succeed with my music. That it wasn't just some hobby for me."

"You certainly did that. You should be so proud of your success and tell us both to kiss your ass."

"I could never do that. That's just not the kind of person I am." He is so right. I could never picture him telling me or his father that, but I wouldn't blame him if he did. I deserved it. We both did. "It's a lonely life if you don't have good people around you. People are so fake when fame hits. The only real family I've got now is my band. These guys are my brothers. They know what all this is like."

"When's the last time you spoke with your folks?"

"I haven't talked with my dad since the night he threw me out four years ago."

"That's awful." My heart breaks for him. "And your mother…"

"Nah, Mom's cool. She sneaks around and calls and emails me when she can. If it weren't for her sneaking me money that first year I was on my own, I probably would have starved to death. Believe me, those cheap, shitty, little noodles are the best meals ever when you're starving and poor."

"I always wondered how rock stars stayed so skinny with all the beer they drink. The starvation diet should be marketed," I say, trying to lighten his mood.

He laughs. "You should totally head that up." The tension seems to melt away a little from his voice, with my joke. I want to ask him a million things. There are so many questions that still linger in my mind about the possibility of fixing their relationship. Some day I hope he'll feel comfortable enough to share everything with me again, just like he used to. But for now, I'll take whatever intimacies about his life he's willing to give me without pushing the issue too much.

Chapter 7

The plane touches down smoothly at Columbus
International Airport. I've never been to Ohio before, never
had a reason to before now. Black Falcon is one of the
headliners of a huge two day rock festival here. Noel
assured me this is the largest rock event in the area. The
sell out crowd is right around fifty thousand people. The
sheer volume alone is crazy.

I grab my bag from the overhead bin after I text
Noel that I've arrived. He insisted on picking me up
himself even though I told him I'm cool with taking a cab
since my flight arrived early in the morning—well, at least
early for rockers who sleep until noon.

My phone chirps, and I read his message. "I'm at
baggage claim. It's crazy here. Don't answer anything they
ask you."

Two women ahead of me on the escalator to the
baggage claim complain about the crowd gathered around
the carousel.

Camera flashes illuminate the center of the mob,
and my heart thumps against my ribs. There he is, signing
autographs and shaking hands with the people surrounding

him. Noel's dark hair is wild, sticking up in every crazy direction, like he just got out of bed. What is it about crazy rocker hair that is so incredibly sexy?

Dark glasses shield his face and emotions from his steady stream of onlookers, but I can tell he's flustered with the whole situation. I guess I didn't realize how little privacy he actually has.

Zero.

He can't even go to the airport without a frenzy of fans.

Noel glances up from the chaos and notices me on the escalator. A huge smile spreads across his face. I feel myself grin and I instantly want to kick myself.

Keep it together, Lanie.

It's undeniable how attractive he is—even more in person than on the net or TV. The entire flock of girls in our high school crushed on him. Back then, I'd never figured out why he was so into me when he could have had any girl he wanted. I'm a Plain Jane—a nobody. Now that feeling is magnified times a million.

He squeezes through his adoring fans. A couple of girls shove their chests against him when he tries to get past in attempts to gain his attention, but it doesn't faze him. Noel watches me with every step he takes.

His arm wraps around my waist and pulls me tight against his chest when I step off the moving stairs. He smells so good, like soap, spice and man all rolled into one. "Hey you," Noel whispers in my ear, and his hot breath caresses my sensitive skin. "Don't say a word to the leeches, okay."

I nod, and the rough stubble along his jaw rubs against my cheek.

We gather my luggage off the carousel, and Noel slings my duffle bag over his shoulder and picks up my suitcase before we head toward the exit. Bodies shove from every direction, all to get closer to Noel. The air is heavy, and my chest tightens. The sooner I can get out of here the better.

What do these people want?

The female fans are relentless—screaming and begging for pictures even when Noel politely tells them not now. The men with high-tech cameras keep shouting his name and asking him to look their way. A crowd smothers our every step.

Noel's long fingers find my hand and pull me against him. It takes us longer than five minutes to make it outside where a black SUV waits by the door. We're quickly greeted by the large man I saw at the restaurant in

New York as he holds the fans back. Noel opens the trunk and throws my bags in before ushering me inside the vehicle.

When the driver pulls the SUV away from the corner, Noel lets out a sigh of relief, and then pats my leg. His skin on mine is so warm and inviting, which is very dangerous. "Sorry about that. I should've had security come in with me, but I figured fans wouldn't see me if I just ran in to get you."

I shove his hand off my bare thigh, and curse myself for wearing shorts. "It's fine."

His eyes gaze into mine as he leans his head back against the headrest. "You made it through your first surprise fan attack. Think you can handle all this? My life isn't exactly sane anymore."

The expression on his face is serious. He's testing if I can put up with his new craziness and make it on this tour for two whole weeks. I inspect my arms under his stare. "I escaped your mob of female admirers without one scratch, so I think I'll live."

Noel grins—clearly pleased with my answer—and leans in and kisses my cheek. "I've missed you."

Warmth spreads clear down to my toes. The things a simple kiss from this man can do to me are unreal. It should be against the law for someone to be so hot and sweet. It's definitely an instant panty wetting combination.

Damn it. I'm in trouble.

"Kisses aren't very professional, Noel."

He bursts out in laughter and pats my thigh again. "I kind of like this whole hard-to-get game. It's going to make the sex that much better."

I remove his hand from me and shake my head. He isn't going to give up.

When we arrive at the Crew Stadium a few minutes later, my eyes widen at the number of people milling about at ten o'clock in the morning. "Why are they all here so early?"

Noel instructs the driver to Black Falcon's tour bus. "There are forty-four bands here total playing in two days. The first band plays at noon today. It's one massive party for both the bands and the fans. There aren't many events like this one."

The SUV pulls up along side the tour bus, and Noel hops out. I sit there frozen. Do I get out now? This is so not my element.

Noel waves at a couple tattooed guys I recognize from the gaggle of Black Falcon pictures I've seen. He walks around to the passenger side of the vehicle and opens my door. "Come on. I want you to meet some of the guys in the band."

I take Noel's outstretched hand and allow him to help me out. Butterflies tumble around in my stomach. How could I be so nervous? I should have prepared myself more for meeting these guys. What if they totally hate the idea of me staying on the bus with them?

We approach the two men—my hand still in Noel's firm grasp. I try to pull away, but he tightens his hold. It's apparent I'm not getting away from him.

The guy with jet black hair and a bandanna tied around his head looks up and elbows the blonde guy. They both grin as we approach.

"You didn't tell us she was unbelievably hot, Noel," bandanna guy says.

My eyes drop down to the ground, and I run my hand through my hair. I can't believe he just called me hot. No guy has ever called me hot to my face before. Well, other than Noel, but we have history together. Most guys just refer to me as cute or pretty, but never hot. Are all rock stars so freaking forward?

Noel punches the guy in the shoulder. "Don't be a douche, Trip. Lane, this asshole is Trip Douglas, one of the best drummers in the business."

Trip shakes my hand and glances sideways at Noel with a cocky grin. "*The* best fucking drummer in the business."

The blonde guy beside Trip chuckles and looks at me. "Noel's right. Trip is kind of an asshole. But, unfortunately, I've always had to put up with him. Tyke Douglas." Tyke holds out his hand. "The asshole is my brother. My twin actually, but please don't hold that against me. And, oh yeah, I play bass in the band."

I smile at both of them. Now that he mentioned twins, I can totally see the resemblance. The stark contrasts of hair color make them look completely different. Noel's hand grazes the skin on the small of my back. "Lanie Vance. It's very nice to meet you both."

Tyke looks at Noel. "She's too sweet. You sure you want to bring her on that bus with us?"

Trip laughs. "Especially around Riff. You better not turn your back, bro. He'll be all over that shit."

Riff, the lead guitarist, is a well-known womanizer. He is the ultimate definition of rock star. He's covered in tattoos and piercings. And his Mohawk alternates between blonde and black. It's really crazy, but the girls seem to go nuts over it. There are always pictures of Riff licking, kissing, or *whatevering* strippers and randomly naked groupies on the internet. He's kind of disgusting. Riff's antics are one of the main reasons the band got so much attention at first, but lately Noel's been making more headlines in that area.

The Douglas brothers obviously don't know that I would never go for someone like that.

Noel tenses next to me. "Riff knows better. Lane is off limits."

Trip and Tyke look at each other with raised eyebrows. I get the distinct feeling that Riff knows no boundaries from the looks on their faces. Whatever they're thinking, it isn't going to happen. I am not having sex on this bus with Riff…or anyone for that matter.

We say our goodbyes to the guys and grab my bags from the SUV. Noel insists on carrying them into the bus.

He stretches out his arm and invites me up the steps. "Welcome aboard Big Bertha."

Big Bertha is a mess. It's a huge R.V. with a full sitting area and cluttered kitchen—beer cans stacked everywhere. The sink is full of dishes, and the garbage can is stuffed to the brim. The stench makes my stomach turn. The mixture of sweaty man and rotten food is evident within the first couple of seconds I'm inside. It's almost bad enough to make me want to turn around and run off this bus. I could follow them in a car, couldn't I?

"Now, I know what your thinking, but I promise you we'll get it cleaned up. It's not always this bad. Being on the road without stopping much tends to make the place a disaster." He smiles at me. "Come on. Let's take your bags to my bedroom."

I freeze mid-step. "You're bedroom? I thought you were kidding when you said that at dinner the other night."

"Where else would you sleep? The other four bunks are taken, unless you want to sleep in one of the swivel seats up front. Trust me. My room is the best place. Come on." He grabs my hand and pulls me toward the back of the bus.

I follow Noel down the hallway. "The bunk beds with curtains are where the other guys in the band sleep, and my bodyguard, Mike. Being the leader of the band gives me specific right to the only bedroom on the bus."

I roll my eyes. I'm sure he shoves his status in their faces anytime he can, just like he does to me.

We step inside the bedroom and I'm surprised by its tidiness. The full size bed takes up most of the room, but there's some stage drawers built into the walls and under the bed for clothes.

"Put your clothes wherever you can find room. I know it's tight in here, but it's better than sleeping in the little foxholes. They can make anyone feel claustrophobic." He shuts the door, trapping us inside the bedroom, and wraps his arms around me. I tense within his arms as I breathe in the spicy scent and the unmistakable smell of Noel. "Now that I have you all to myself, let me give you a proper hello."

I place my hand against his chest. "This isn't how it's going to work, Noel. I didn't agree to this deal to be your private sex slave."

He backs me against the door and places a hand on either side of me, effectively trapping me. My arm feels like Jell-o as I try to hold him back. I swallow hard as he leans in and traces his nose along the length of my jaw line. "Sex Slave? Hmmmmm, I kind of like the sound of that."

I shove him back a little and shake my head. "Don't get any ideas. That isn't happening. I came here for business, remember?"

He threads his fingers into my hair. "I don't see why we can't mix a little pleasure in too. Don't you remember how hot we were together, Lane? *God.*" He takes in a quick breath through clenched teeth and runs his hand down my side, "The things I can do to your body if you'd let me."

The nerves inside my body jitter. Noel's skin is so warm, and I swear he's leaving a trail of fire in his wake. Fire spreads from my core causing an ache I didn't know is possible. I've dreamt of his touch for the last four years. I want this so much, but I can't let this happen. If I give into him now, he'll tire of me quicker and not only will my heart break, but my dreams for a killer job will be crushed.

He reaches out and takes a strand of my brown hair between his fingers. The corners of his lips turn up, and he tucks the loose strand behind my ear. His fingertips linger on my cheek. "You look exactly the same. Still the most beautiful girl I've ever seen." He brings his lips toward mine. Warmth from his breath touches my face, and all I can think about is his kiss. What it will feel like. Will it be just like old times?

"You don't look so bad yourself." My heart thunders with anticipation, and I bite my lip.

"You know I've never been great at resisting beautiful women." Noel's eyes search my face.

I should tell him to back off. It will be smart to say no right away, but I stare deep into his blue eyes and I can't kid myself. I want him more than I've ever wanted anything in my entire life. Resisting him is so damn hard. "I—I don't think—"

Noel cradles my face in both hands. A smile flirts along his lips. "Don't think, Lane, just feel."

That's the problem. If I feel too much for him this won't end well. I can't let this happen. "We should really get to work."

He rubs his nose against mine. "One kiss and I'll behave all day."

I swallow hard and try to pretend the mere touch of his skin against mine isn't sending my body into overdrive. If he only knew the effect he's having on me right now. It's been far too long since I'd been with a guy—over a year, actually. He's lucky I don't strip him down here and now.

I shake the last thought out of my head, and Noel pulls back a little.

I swallow hard. "That can't happen between us. I don't have those kinds of feeling for you anymore."

He raises an eyebrow and his grin turns wicked. "Are you sure about that? Don't forget, Lane, I know you. I know how you tick and what you…"—his eyes scan the length of my body, lingering on my breasts—"want."

Damn him. I shove against his chest. "You're wrong."

Noel laughs as he pushes himself away from the wall and gestures me further into the room. "Well if you're sure you don't require any further assistance from me, I'll leave you to it. But…if you change your mind—"

"I won't," I snap, cutting him off and step past him. I can't even look at the smug expression I know he's wearing.

He chuckles while he lets himself out the bedroom door and I let out a sigh of relief.

Chapter 8

Five Finger Death Punch rocks out hard on the stage and the audience is insane. I count at least five mosh pits not far from the front row. Girls sit on guys' shoulders and flash their bare breasts at the band on stage while the crowd hollers encouragements to egg them on. Some must've gotten tired of tops altogether and sit there without a shirt while rocking out.

Crazy.

There's some sort of wild energy in the air that has everyone hyped. Even I feel it as I bob my head to the beat. Now I know what Noel is talking about. This is a major rock event, and everyone is enjoying themselves to the fullest. There's some sort of spell that sucks you into the moment going on here.

Backstage is busy as well. There are people everywhere I turn. A few of the bands I recognize off music videos or tour posters I've seen Black Falcon on before, but the rest of the people are faceless strangers. A few giddy female fans mill about and gush over their favorite bands, and I smile every time I hear one of them mention Noel's band. Those girls don't bother me much. They seem harmless. I don't think they're back here to attempt to get in the band member's pants.

The hardcore groupies and strippers, on the other hand, have a different agenda. It's like they're on a mission to get laid by the most famous guy that will have them. A few of them have even hit on the female rockers that are backstage. Pathetic, really. What would drive a woman to want to be used for sex by someone so badly? They must have some serious Daddy issues.

A large crowd gathers by the steps that lead up to the stage area where I am. Cameras flash, and I strain my neck hoping Noel's back from his band meeting. People cram in tight, pushing to gain every inch they can toward their target. Riff makes it to the top step while he signs autographs and kisses some of his female admirers. I sigh—still no Noel yet. I tilt my head, curious as to what it is about Riff that drives the girls wild.

I just can't figure it out.

Sure he's really cute, even a blind woman can see that, but that alone wouldn't make me want to sleep with him. Who knows what kind of person he is. I don't judge, but I'm going to sleep with a person based off looks alone.

I'm no slut.

Security cuts the girls off on the stage. "Sorry, ladies, this area is off limits." I hear the wall of muscle tell the girls as he and his partner hold them back. The girls all whine with disappointment and beg to follow Riff.

My eyes dart to Riff, and he smiles when he catches me staring at him. He walks toward me, his eyes never leaving me once.

"Damn, you're sexy," Riff says to me as his eyes rake slowly over my body. His gaze stops directly on my breasts under my tank top. I narrow my eyes at him. He doesn't seem the least bit bothered I have the look of red death pointed directly at him. He pulls a piece of gold paper from his pocket. "This golden ticket grants you access into my pants when our set is over. Hold on to it tight and give it to security that guards the buses. They'll let you through. I only give away one or two of those a night. Consider yourself a lucky lady."

He stuffs the paper into my hands, and I furrow my brows. Is he serious right now? Does he think just because he shoves some gold paper in my hand that I will instantly drop my panties for him? I shake my head and try to hand him back the paper. "No thanks."

"Not interested?" Riff laughs. "Sweetie, that's cute, but you don't have to play hard to get. I know why you're back here, and I can guarantee there's no better time to be had than the one you're going to get with me."

He licks his lip and runs his hand down my arm. His skin on mine makes my blood boil. How dare he think he can just touch me like that?

I slap the paper into his chest. "I'm waiting for someone, you asshole. I'm not some random fucking groupie."

Surprise registers on his face and then a slow grin. "You're feisty. I like that." He tilts his head. "What a shame. We could've been pretty awesome together tonight. You know where to find me if you change your mind."

I huff as Riff lets the piece of paper fall to the ground. It lands by his feet and he smirks at me before he turns and walks away.

What I wouldn't give for murdering someone to be legal right now. I should kill that asshole for the benefit of all womankind.

Noel finds me about ten minutes after my run in with Riff. At first I think about telling Noel, but decide against it. Their chemistry has to be on point in front of this many people.

I can always tell him about it later. Besides, I'm sure Riff will feel like a jackass when he discovers who I am.

Noel's white t-shirt strains against his chest and biceps as he wraps his arms around me. "Are you going to watch my set?"

I try to pull his arms away from my waist, but Noel grins, and squeezes me tighter.

I sigh. "Not if you keep manhandling me like this."

His laugh rumbles in his chest and our pelvises smash together. "I think if you keep rubbing against me like that, I'm going to take you back to the bus and fuck you right now."

I raise an eyebrow and fight the urge to smack him across his smug face. "You wish. Besides, if you disappoint your fans, they might just fire your conceited ass."

Noel's hands cup my face and leans in for a kiss, but stops just inches from my lips when I resist. He licks his lips. "It might just be worth it."

A laugh escapes me and I immediately cover my mouth with my hand. My eyes widen as I realize I've let my tough shell crack a bit, but he's so damn forward and it's kind of comical.

"Grrrrrr," he growls and pulls me against his warm body. "You know it drives me crazy when you giggle." He cups my butt through my jean shorts and presses the bulge in his pants against me. "See what you did? How am I supposed to go in front of fifty thousand people like this?"

I laugh and pull away from him. "Not my problem. You'll just have to hide it behind your guitar."

An impatient stage manager appears out of no where. "Noel, we need you in position."

Noel takes a heavy breath. "Okay, gotta go. See you after we're done."

He smiles and heads toward the stage. Another giggle bubbles out of me when he readjusts his pants and picks up his guitar. Poor Noel. Smug satisfaction, mixing with a little guilt, surges through me.

My eyes glue onto Noel's backside until he's out of sight. I must admit his butt is really nice. Okay, okay—it's damn near perfect. No wonder he has so many women lusting after him.

The crowd rumbles as they chant for Black Falcon to take the stage. It's not surprising considering people really love Noel's band. They're one of the most played bands on the charts. Noel's dream of millions of people hearing his music has most definitely arrived. Some critics say they could be one of the next greats. Throwing them in line with bands like, The Beatles, Queen, Aerosmith— bands that changed the face of music.

I always knew Noel was great, but I guess I never realized how great until the rest of the world discovered him. It's like he walks on water to his fans.

This band is his life now, and I couldn't be happier he allowed me back into his world, considering I dumped him after graduation.

I take a couple steps toward the stage. It's definitely the best spot in the stadium to watch a Black Falcon performance. A woman with bright, red hair whom I recognize from the music video channel, steps out on to the stage. She's this weekend's host and hops from stage to stage introducing the bands. The crowd roars as she waves to them wearing her skin-tight black, leather pants and halter top.

She brings the mic up to her lips and asks, "Are you fuckers ready for one of the best damn bands at this festival!"

I scream along with the crowd to answer her question.

"These guys are one of my personal favorites, not to mention they look pretty fucking amazing, too. Right, ladies?" She pauses and allows for crowd reaction. "Give it up for BLACK FALCON!"

Trip takes the stage first and throws up a metal sign. People scream at the black-haired rocker as he takes his seat and gives the bass drum a kick. Tyke comes out second and picks up his bass guitar. Screams erupt when he thumps a couple cords out. The two twin brothers look at each other and smile like they have an inside secret, and it drives the fans nuts.

Riff and Noel come onstage together. My eardrums feel like they are about to explode from the sheer volume in this stadium. Noel glances my way on the side of the stage, and I wave to him. Riff, still clueless, smirks at me and wiggles his tongue while his back is to Noel.

Dear God, does this asshole think I'm here for him?

I roll my eyes at Riff, and he smiles before he puckers his lips at me. He just doesn't get it and won't take no for an answer.

The band kicks up and plays their intro song. I do my best to stare past Riff and watch Noel perform, but every time Riff sees me he makes sexual gestures of some kind—once even thrusting his hips while stroking his guitar. The crowd loves it, of course, but my stomach is about five seconds from losing the bagel I ate on the airplane.

Noel leans into the mic and wraps both hands around it. He licks his lips and closes his eyes. The red stage light on him causes something in me to stir. It's like it's highlighting him as the most sexually pleasing man I know. My knees buckle when his voice belts out a love song. The audience sings along to every word. I sway to the beat, but never take my eyes off of him.

Something flies up on stage at Noel's feet. I look down and realize it's a thong. These women are actually throwing their disgusting panties at him. Several more join the first one at Noel's feet.

Riff steps up to his mic. "That's what I like to see. Horny women! Damn." He points out. "You fuckers better not let all that pussy go to waste. Now show me some titties."

Men throughout the place cheer and chant. "GET NAKED! GET NAKED!"

A couple girls near the front row climb onto guys' shoulders and rip off their tops and shake their boobs at Riff and Noel. My hands clench in fists, and I have half the mind to go yank them down and ask just where do they get off shoving their breasts in Noel's face?

But thankfully Noel just shakes his head at Riff and laughs. The muscles in my body relax a little. I remind myself that this is part of Noel's life. It's all an act. It isn't like he'll be screwing around with those girls later just because they flashed him, will he? I know I walked in on him with those two sluts back in Houston, but I don't think he'd do that now that I'm here. Would he?

Riff, on the other hand, I'm not so sure about. There were several times I'd spoken to Noel after a show and he told me Riff had some random groupie in the foxhole with him. Sometimes I could even hear the girl screaming in pleasure. It was disgusting.

Riff glances at Noel and points at one topless girl and nods his head. "Now that's what I'm talking about!"

I shake my head, again. Riff is a complete sex fiend. The only reason he's in a band is probably for the women.

Noel's smooth voice shoots out over the crowd. I close my eyes. It's like a beautiful lullaby. For a hard-rock band, they could sure play a sweet ballad.

I open my eyes, and my gaze locks on Noel's eyes. He sings into the mic about the love of a good woman and I feel a blush creep up my neck. When the chorus hits, he breaks our stare and faces the audience. Cell phones light up across the sea of people and they dance like fireflies in the dusk.

The song ends, and the crowd roars until Trip pounds out a fast beat on the drums. Tyke and Riff join in, and the song zings to life.

Noel's voice changes to his signature growl he likes to use when the band rocks out. He yanks the mic off the stand and bends at the waist to belt out a note. The crowd hypes up when he runs from one corner of the stage to the next. Girls stretch out their arms, hoping to touch him, and guys reach out for a high-five.

Everyone wants a piece of him.

The song ends, but the guys play an extra few bars on the song to allow Noel time to thank the crowd before they wrap up their set.

Tyke waves to the fans before he heads behind the stage. Riff throws out guitar picks, and Trip wings his sticks out to the people in the back. Noel wipes his face with a white hand towel before he tosses it into the mass of people. There are about ten fans that shove and grab for the towel before one lucky guy yanks it into his grasp.

The life of a rock star is unreal.

Big Bertha is quiet when Noel and I climb inside, which is a relief after we just fought our way through a ton of screaming women on the other side of security. Those guys in the yellow shirts have to put up with a lot of crap to protect the stars.

Noel's sweat drenched shirt clings to his sculpted chest. His normal fohawk is a flat disaster. "I need to go shower. I'll only be a few minutes. Wait for me right here?"

He brings my right hand up to his lips and kisses my fingertips. A rush of warmth spreads through me before I pull them away. "I'm not going anywhere."

Noel grins at me before he rushes off toward the small bathroom on the bus.

My stomach rumbles because I've forgotten to eat during the midst of this crazy day. I step over to the kitchen area and open a couple of top cabinet doors. No food. What do these guys live on? Beer? I bend down to check the bottom shelves.

"I knew you'd be here." I slam the door shut and stand to face Riff. "The ladies never turn down the golden ticket."

Riff's arm stretches above his head as he balances his weight against a top cabinet. He's shirtless, and I can clearly see the tattoos across his arms and chest. Both of his nipples are pierced along with his bottom lip and his hair still stands in his trademark Mohawk.

A slow grin pulls across his face as I pull at the legs of my shorts, hoping to cover some more skin. His eyes trace the curves of my body as he pulls his arm down and takes a step.

I hold out my hand palm up. "Stop right there."

Riff reaches out for my hand, but I snatch it away from his grasp. "Baby, I told you. No need to play hard to get. I won't tell anyone that you fucked me."

My eyes widen at his audacity. "You're really full of yourself, you know that?"

He smirks. "Only when it comes to women."

I roll my eyes. "I hate to be the one to break it to you, but not every woman on the planet is willing to sleep with you, Riff."

"Maybe." He shrugs. "But I can tell that *you* want me." He takes another step toward me and I try to back away from his advance only to bump against the cabinets behind me.

I shove my hand into his chest and shake my head. "No, I don't want you. I'm here with—"

"Shhhhhhhhhhhhh." Riff strokes the skin on my shoulder. "No more talking."

"What the fuck do you think you're doing, Riff?" Noel growls from the hallway, wearing a low-slung towel around his hips, while water beads speckle his chest. Riff jumps at the sound of Noel's voice.

Riff releases me and takes a step back. His eyes lock on my face. "You're Lanie?"

I nod and glance at Noel. "I've tried to tell you. I told you I was with someone when you first tried to shove that ticket thing in my hand."

Noel's eyes narrow at Riff. "You gave her one of your fucking Golden Tickets? I'm going to fucking kill you."

Noel lunges at Riff, but he reacts just quick enough to stay out of Noel's grasp and shove his hands away.

I throw my hands against Noel's chest. "It's okay. Let it go. He made a mistake." I point my stare at Riff. "Right?"

Riff stares Noel down. "Yeah, we wouldn't want to accidently steal each other's woman, would we?"

Riff's tone makes me flinch.

The muscle in Noel's jaw clenches. "You stay away from her. Or so help me God, Riff, I will end you."

I swallow hard. I've never seen a look of pure malice until now. Noel expression and body language clearly says he wants to rip Riff's head off and spit down his throat. This tension between them can't honestly be about me, can it? It feels more personal than just a case of mistaken identity.

Riff and Noel continue to stare each other down. There's obviously some bad history between these two, and I've just added fuel to the fire. Something has to give. I can't let the band struggle because of me. This situation needs to be diffused.

I pull on Noel's arm and he tilts his head and gazes down at me. "Come on, Noel. I want to show you something." I grab his hand in mine and tug him toward the bedroom.

Noel stares at Riff, like he's debating on if he should just pummel him now and get it over with. Finally, he nods and follows me down the hallway, leaving Riff alone in the front of the bus.

He sits on the edge of the bed while I close the door. He drops his head down and combs his hand through this thick, dark hair. The bed gives a little under my weight when I sit beside him. His back is smooth and clean as I run my fingers along it in attempts to comfort him. The smell soap lingers on his skin. He doesn't respond to my touch—his gaze points toward the floor.

I stare at the star tattoo he has on his right shoulder. "It's going to be okay. He didn't realize who I am and I doubt he'll do it again."

Noel rubs the palms of his hands together. "You don't know him like I do. Riff doesn't stop until he gets what he wants, which includes women. I won't let him use you like that."

I want to laugh. Doesn't he know me at all? "He's not going to get me, Noel. I'm not like the random sluts he's used to seeing you with."

Blue eyes meet mine. "No, you're not." He searches my face and his brow pulls in. He opens his mouth to say something, then closes it quickly and turns away. "You better get ready. One hell of a party is about to go down."

Chapter 9

I wiggle a bit between Noel and Riff in the back of the SUV on the way to this humongous afterparty for all the bands who performed at *Rock on the Range* this weekend. The A&R Music Bar here in Columbus hosts the bash to millionaire bad-boy rock stars, roadies, and of course, their groupies.

It takes forever to get close to the building. Hoards of people surround the building hoping to catch a glimpse of their favorite rock stars, and are blocking traffic half way down the street.

When the vehicle finally stops near the back entrance, Mike, Noel's bodyguard from the restaurant, hops out and opens the door for us. Trip and Tyke grin at each other before emerging into the mass of fans. They love the attention. They hug several of the screaming female fans and even stop to sign a couple bare boobs thrusting in their direction.

Riff looks at me and winks before he jumps out.

I roll my eyes. Of course he would love this.

I slide over to follow Riff, and Noel lays his hand on top of mine. "Stay by me in here. Shit like this gets crazy. Don't accept drinks from anyone other than me or Mike. There are real assholes in there that would love to get in your pants."

I raise my eyebrow. "They can't be any worse than you."

His mouth pulls into a tight line. "You have no idea."

Inside the club, it appears like something out of a music video. Bodies writhe everywhere to the beat of the rock song echoing throughout the room. Strobe lights flash in every direction, and women wearing bikinis dance in cages. One next to me reaches through the bars and strokes my arm with her fingertips. Her touch catches me off guard and I instinctively jerk away. Noel chuckles beside me.

I narrow my eyes at him. "So not funny."

His smile widens. "Get used to it, babe. When you're with me, everyone's going to want a piece of you."

"Gross."

He throws his arms around me and leans into my ear. "What's it like to know you're with the one guy in this room every woman wants to fuck?"

I shove him out of my ear. "Not every woman."

I storm away from him. Even over the blaring music, I can hear his laugh behind me and I clench my fists tight. I don't remember him being so stuck on himself.

I step up to the bar and order a beer.

"Trouble in paradise?" I glance over to find Riff beside me, leaning against the bar.

Great. I'm so not in the mood for another jackass.

I roll my eyes and take the beer from the smiling brunette woman behind the counter. "No trouble…and definitely no paradise. This is just a job for me."

"Ah, the charity, right?" Riff's brown eyes twinkle as he watches me. "How's that going?"

I pick at the label on the bottle in my hand. "Pretty much non-existent at the moment. Noel keeps putting off hammering out the details about the literacy program. That's the whole reason I'm here—to get the marketing off the ground."

Riff nods. "He's thinking ahead, I'll give him that."

"What do you mean?"

"He's going to string you along for as long as he can until he gets what he wants from you. The more information he gives you about the project the band has going on, the sooner you can leave and go back to New York. I know you two have some history, so you're a challenge to him. That's a game he hasn't had to play for quite some time. He tends to always get what he wants."

I shake my head. "Yeah, well, what he wants from me, he isn't going to get."

He smiles. "That's good to know." He nods toward the dance floor. "want to dance?"

I turn towards the sea of people and my eyes fixate on a couple practically molesting each other on the floor, right in plain view of everyone in the club. They grind their pelvises together, leaving little to the imagination of what a night in their bedroom would be like. How can people do that in public? I shake my head. "Um, no, thanks."

He runs his fingers along my arm, and I tense. "Come on, Lanie. I won't bite."

I shake my head, and before I can answer, I'm being dragged away by the other arm. Noel's eyes are hard when he looks back at Riff. The appearance of pure hate doesn't seem to faze Riff, though. He simply lifts his beer in the air and gives Noel a small nod. Why do I feel like I'm in the middle of a childish game of tug-of-war?

I yank free of Noel's grip. "What the hell?"

Noel's expression darkens. "I told you to stay away from him."

My arms fold over my chest. I'm ready for a fight. "I'm a big girl, Noel. I can talk to whomever I want."

He turns away as he runs his hand through his hair. He opens his mouth like he wants to say something, then immediately closes it. I stare at him, waiting for his smart ass reply, but after a couple seconds, he turns back to me and holds out his hand. "Dance with me."

I flinch. "What? Are you psycho? There's medication for that, you know."

Before I can think, he grabs me up into his arms against his chest. "Psycho…no…a little crazy…maybe." He leans into my ear and says with a slight growl, "Dance with me."

The words cause my stomach to clench. I know he's trying to break me down. The minute I give into him and let him touch my body, it will want him. And I hate that he knows that.

I shove his chest, putting personal space between us again, and take a long drink from my beer. Dancing with him definitely crosses the line. "No."

His brow furrows. "No?"

Noel obviously doesn't hear that word very often. "I'm here on business, not to…" I gesture towards the crowd. "Let you grind all up on me."

Before he can say another word, I walk away from him and take an empty seat at the end of the bar. Noel watches me for a second, like he's debating whether to follow me or not, but I refuse to acknowledge his existence. Eventually, he gives up and heads toward the table the twins occupy. As soon as his ass hits the seat, a perky blonde plops down in his lap. He wraps his arm around her waist and takes a long pull from his beer bottle. She whispers in his ear and he nods and gives her that sexy-cocky grin I'm starting to hate.

I tear my eyes away just as the girl leans in and kisses his lips. I grip my bottle a little too tight and narrow my eyes. Then it hits me on why I feel so angry, and I can't believe it. I'm actually a little jealous.

I chug down the rest of my beer and try to drown out the thought. What Noel and I had was in the past, and I have no right to feel that way when he's with someone in front of me now.

A man who resembles a younger version of Steven Tyler takes the seat next to me and orders a beer before turning his attention to me. A blush creeps up my neck when I turn to find him watching me intently. His lips turn up into a smile, and I retrain my eyes back on the bottle in front of me.

The man shoves a strand of his long, black hair behind his ear. "You need another?"

His accent is delicious. There's something about a British accent that's incredibly sexy.

I nod. "Sure."

Mr. Accent gestures for another beer, and I study his features. His black hair hangs nearly to his broad shoulders, and his tattooed hands poke out from the long sleeved shirt he's wearing. Both of his ears are pierced along with one eyebrow, and his eyes are deep chocolate. He's obviously in a band, most guys in here are, but I can't put my finger on which one.

He turns toward me and holds out his hand. "I'm Striker."

Ah. That's where I've seen him. He's the front man of Embrace the Darkness.

I slide my hand in his. "Lanie Vance."

The bartender returns with the drink and winks at the rocker as she sets it down in front of him.

"Here you go, love," he says and slides the bottle in my direction. "So, what's a beautiful lady like you doing in here with this lot?"

I blush again and run my fingers through my hair. "I'm working."

He raises his eyebrows. "Blimey! You're a…"

My eyes widen as I realize his mistake. "No!" I nudge his hand. "No. I'm not a…you know. I'm a rep for Center Stage Marketing."

"Right, I've heard of them—out of New York. My record label suggested we look into using them." He nods and smiles. "Here to pick up new clients then?"

I lean closer to his ear so my voice doesn't compete with the blaring music. "I'm actually working for Black Falcon on their children's literacy campaign."

"They make you travel to this shithole town in Ohio for that? Seems like rubbish to me," he says in my ear.

I shrug. "Noel and I are old friends. He kind of got me this job."

He touches my hand this time when he speaks. "Well, an old friend of Noel's, can I get your name and maybe give you a ring sometime?"

I take a sip of my drink. There's nothing wrong with giving him my number, right? It's not like I'm dating anyone or anything. Besides this guy seems cute and genuinely interested in getting to know me. "I'd like that."

The rocker picks up his beer and clinks it with mine after he stuffs my cell number in his front, jean pocket. "To new friends."

"There something you need, Striker?" Noel says behind me.

I turn on the stool. Noel stands there with his arms across his chest as he stares at the back of Striker's head.

My eyes flick to Striker, and he lets out a slow breath as he turns around and stands. He chugs the last of his beer and sits the bottle on the counter, like he's in no hurry. "No, mate. I've got all I need right here." He pats the front pocket he slid my number into and promptly turns his attention to me. "Lanie, love, it's been charming. We'll be in touch."

Striker shoulders past Noel without another look in his direction and blends into the crowd of people in the club.

"What the hell are you drinking?" Noel grabs the beer out of my hands and chucks it in a nearby trash can. "I told you not to take drinks from anyone but me."

"You're infuriating. You know that." I jump off the stool and head towards the exit in desperate need for space, but he grabs my arm. "Let me go."

He shakes his head. "You want to leave? Then we'll go together."

I yank away. "Fine. Let's go, then."

Mike holds the crowd off so we can hop into the SUV. Noel slams the door shut and the vehicle quivers a little. His mouth pulls into a tight line and he runs his fingers through his hair. He seems frustrated.

I know the feeling.

Neither of us speak the entire ride back to Big Bertha. The minute we step on to the bus, Noel flops down in the sitting area near the door and picks up his guitar. He strums out random chords and does his best not to make eye contact with me.

After watching him for about twenty seconds, I finally get that he's not going to talk about what happened at the club and why he feels like he has the right to dictate who I talk to. A harsh breath escapes me, and I storm into the bedroom. Once inside, I take off my top then grab an oversized t-shirt from the drawer I stuffed all my clothes in earlier today and yank it over my head.

Where does he get off being such an asshole to me? If he doesn't want me here, he shouldn't have made it mandatory for me to come.

I burst through the door and then go directly into the bathroom, without a glance in Noel's direction, to scrub the make-up from my face and get ready for bed. I tug a brush through my unruly, dark waves and pull it up into a high bun on the top of my head.

When I return to the back room, I freeze in the doorway. Noel lies on the bed with his arms tucked behind his head, while from the waist down he's under the covers. The tattoos on his naked chest and arms are beautiful. They make him look so anti-authority and bad-boyish. I wish it wasn't so ridiculously sexy.

I throw my hands up. "Hello? What are you doing back here?"

He furrows his eyebrows like I'm not speaking English. "What do you mean, why am I back here? It's my room."

I fold my arms over my chest. "Yes, but when you told me earlier that I'd be sleeping in your bed, I didn't think you meant with you in it."

Noel shrugs. "I told you there wasn't any room in the foxholes. I thought I made the sleeping arrangements very clear."

"I'm not sleeping back here with you!"

He raises an eyebrow. "If you want to sleep in on one of the seats out front, be my guest. But I warn you, the other guys never come home alone, and most of the action takes place right up front."

I turn and peer down the hall at the two swivel seats and tiny love seat and shudder. No way do I want to witness the guys' sexual escapades out there. I sigh and drop my arms. "Fine. But so help me, if you touch me, I'll punch you square in the balls."

He laughs and pats the spot beside him. "I'll be a gentleman. I promise."

Reluctantly, I walk over and slide under the covers next to Noel. The full size bed doesn't exactly leave much space between us, so I scoot as close to the edge as I can get and roll on my side away from him.

The light flicks off, and the bed shakes as Noel settles down on his pillow. It's quiet. Too quiet actually. With nothing to distract me, all I can think about is how close his body is to mine. How if I wanted, I could roll over and have amazing sex with this man.

I tuck the cover around me and close my eyes. Right before I drift into sleep after an exhausting day, Noel says, "I'm sorry about tonight, Lane. I shouldn't allow myself to get so jealous. You're a hard one to let go."

My heart pounds, and I'm suddenly fully awake. There are a million things I can say to him. But if I'm not careful, one sentence can either piss him off or turn him on and neither of those would be a good thing.

We lay there in silence, but I can't bring myself to say anything. Noel eventually takes the hint and lets out a heavy sigh before he turns over and doesn't speak a single word.

Chapter 10

My cell rings on the small night stand, and my eyes pop open. Relief engulfs me when I roll over and see the other half of the bed empty. I grab the phone and answer it as I sit up and run my fingers through my tangled bed-head.

"Good morning, sunshine." Aubrey says in a sing-song voice.

"What time is it?" I question and flop back on my pillow. The motions of the moving bus are steady and very sleep inducing. Must be why I slept so late.

She laughs into the phone. "Someone had a late night? It's nearly noon. Tell me, any action with that sexy rocker yet?"

"Ugh. You would not believe what that asshole said to me last night."

I rehash all the grimy details of how it seems like Noel is a crazy lunatic only interested in getting into my pants. Of course, I leave out the details about how amazingly hot he is when he becomes so suggestive because knowing Aubrey, she'll encourage me to take him up on the offers because she knows it's been a while for me in that department.

"So tomorrow my flight comes into Dallas at two thirty. I'm renting a car so I can drive myself over to the hotel while I wait on you to get there."

I sigh. "You don't know how excited I'll be to see a friendly face."

"Pssssssssssh. Whatever. After that story you just told me, sounds like you've been seeing plenty of 'friendly' faces between Noel, Riff, and that sexy British dude."

"You mean Striker?"

She giggles. "I need to Google him, even his name sounds yummy." I hear Aubrey tapping on the keys of the desktop computer in our little apartment and I suddenly feel a little homesick. "Ah, there we go. Let me just…Oh yeah, he's fucking edible. No bag needed for that one's head. That's for sure."

I shake my head. "I doubt he'll ever call me. Noel chased him off before I could make a good impression."

"Noel's just jealo—Oh-my-god, Lanie have you searched your own name in the last twenty-four hours?"

"Um, no. Does anyone really look themselves up that often? Why?"

"Go get your laptop and search your name, and then call me back."

"Wait. Aubrey. Why?"

"Just go do it."

After I promise to call her right back, I hop off the bed and change into a pair of jeans and black t-shirt. I grab my computer from the cabinet and boot it up. I'm surprised to find there's a Big Bertha Wi-Fi signal. After a failed attempt to connect, I make my way out to the front of the bus, laptop in hand, where all the guys are up eating breakfast.

"What's popping, Lanie?" Trip asks before he takes a huge bite of cereal.

Tyke and Riff are locked into some battle on the game system attached to the flat screen TV in the sitting room. Noel sits to the side watching them go at it, ignoring that I'm in the room.

"Trip, what's the Wi-Fi password for Big Bertha?"

He wipes his chin with the sleeve of his shirt and grins. "It's kinkysexgod69."

I roll my eyes. "What is it with you guys and your obsession with sex?"

I sit my laptop on the counter next to Trip's bowl and type in the password. Once it's connected, I type my name into the search engine. A couple milliseconds tick by and my name accompanied by pictures pop up in the results. I click on a picture, and it redirects me to a celebrity gossip site where Noel and I are the prime story with a headline reading: Black Falcon Front Man Caught with Secret Lover. My eyes widen as I take in the picture with Noel holding my hand in the airport.

"Shit," Trips says next to me.

Noel looks up from the game. "What?"

"There's pictures of the two of you on the internet. They are calling our girl Lanie here, your secret lover."

Noel practically leaps from his seat and comes behind Trip and I to check out the screen. "Fuck!" he growls.

I flinch. Am I really that embarrassing to be seen with? How can pretend that he's so into me one minute, and then be pissed cameras have caught us holding hands the next? "What's your problem? It's a harmless picture. Who cares? We both know it isn't true."

He paces in the kitchen a few seconds and then darts up to the front of the bus. Noel doesn't say another word to me. Instead, he rushes past me and into the other room to retrieve his cell phone, and then plops down in the seat next to the driver. Big Bertha takes the next exit and pulls into a truck stop.

I watch as Noel shoves his hands through his hair as he waits by the door for the bus to fully stop.

He's acting like a complete fucking lunatic.

The rest of the guys hop off the bus and then start towards the convenience store. The second I step off the bus I glance around. Noel's at the back of the bus talking on his cell. Whoever he's talking with is obviously arguing with him. I can't make out what he's saying, but the wild gestures his arms are doing tells me he's defending himself.

He takes a breath and his shoulders slump before closing his eyes. Whatever the fight was over, he now looks relieved. Curiosity wins out, and I take another couple steps toward him. Noel notices me and straightens himself as I approach.

Before I can hear more than him say goodbye to the other person on the line, he snaps, "How long have you been there?"

I shake my head. "I wasn't eaves dropping." Okay, so maybe that isn't exactly the truth, but I didn't really hear anything either. "I wanted to make sure you were okay. You rushed out of there so quickly."

Noel stuffs his phone into his back pocket. "Everything's fine—just business—nothing that concerns you."

I flinch at his snippy tone. "Sorry. I was just…concerned."

He sighs and drags his fingers through his messy brown hair. "Fuck! I really feel like all I do is fuck things up when it comes to you. I shouldn't snap at you. It's not your fault I have bad shit in my life. I really don't mean it. I'm sorry."

This is the second time in less than a day Noel has apologized to me. I really don't get how he can be so forward and overly sexual towards me, then flip the switch and tell me he's sorry for hurting me. He's like a man possessed by craziness.

"So…" He closes the space between us and holds out his arms for a hug. "Friends, again?"

I shrug and wrap my arms around his waist. "Friends."

It actually feels good to get to this point. We should be able to be friends without all this weird tension between us. Two people who dated in high school should be able to look past that and have a healthy friendship. This is going to make working on the children's literacy campaign so much easier.

I rest my head against his chest, and he rubs my back. Noel holding me like this reminds me of when we were a couple and he was unbelievably sweet. I sigh and give him one final squeeze before I let this lingering hug between us get weird.

"Come on. I'll buy you some of those sour-lemon candies you like so much." He tugs my shirt.

I grin. It's funny the things people remember about another person. "Only if you eat some with me."

He laughs and throws his arm around me as we start towards the store. "The thought alone of eating those things make me want to puke. I ate what—one hundred and fifty of those things in one sitting because you dared me?"

"It was four hundred and eighty-seven. The bet was five hundred remember? And you lost miserably." I poke his stomach.

He grabs my hand and holds it against his chest over his heart. It's a simple gesture, but a dangerous one. Something so sweet will wear down my willpower to resist him if he tries to tempt me into sleeping with him again. I know the Noel I use to love is in this sexy, bad-boy rocker somewhere.

I pull my hand away, and Noel gazes down at me with sad eyes. Desperate for a subject change I say, "My friend, Aubrey, is meeting up with us in Dallas tomorrow."

"Is she the one that came with you to the show, when you…" His eyes dart away from mine. It's like he doesn't want to bring up the time I walked in on him with the two sluts back in Houston.

Allowing him off the hook, I don't even acknowledge his slip up. "Yeah. She's from Texas, so she's flying down to catch the show and driving to her parents place near Waco when we leave for the next city."

He nods. "We'll actually spend a couple days in Dallas. Our manager booked us all rooms so we can get off the bus for a bit."

A smile creeps across my lips. "You think we'll have time to drive home for a night? I'm sure your parents will be thrilled to see you."

Noel stops in his tracks. "No. I promised myself I'd never go back there, not after the way Dad treated me."

"But your mom…don't you miss her?"

He sighs. "Of course I do."

"Well, then come home with me."

He raises his eyebrows. "What do you mean, come home with you?"

I turn my hands over and shrug. "My parents would love to have you over. We can drive down, invite your mom to dinner at my mom's house, and we can stay the night. It'd give you a chance to spend time with your mom without having to face your father."

"You'd do that for me?"

"Of course I would. You're my oldest friend."

Noel throws his arm around me and pulls me in close to his side just like old times, and I'm amazed how natural it feels.

Chapter 11

We pull into Dallas a little after four o'clock the next day. The bus rounds the corner towards the American Airlines Center concert hall. This is yet another monstrously huge venue Black Falcon will no doubt fill tomorrow night. Security guards open the 'authorized personal only' gate and allow the bus to pass through. The driver turns the bus smoothly into the back lot area and then cuts the engine.

"Whoo hoo! Two days of freedom, boys!" Trip yells as he slaps a baseball cap over his jet black hair. "Now to find me a little honey while I'm here."

Tyke laughs at his brother as he looks out the bus window. "That shouldn't be a problem."

I follow his line of sight. A mass of fans wait outside with cameras and 'We love you' signs in hand. Most of them are women, but there are a few guys in the mix as well. The majority seems harmless, but a handful of women stick out in their scantily clad clothing that screams 'fuck me!' Trip and Tyke point out a few and chat amongst themselves calling dibs on certain women.

Riff joins them and gives the group a careful once over, like he's deciding on which dessert to pick.

I roll my eyes.

Men.

My cell phone rings, and I yank it from my back pocket. "I was just getting ready to call you."

"Good thing because I'm already here," Aubrey says into the phone. "I think this is the bus your on."

I shove in-between the gawking men and scan the crowd. Aubrey stands to the side with the phone against her ear wearing a pair of low rise cut off shorts and a black tank top. She's showing just enough stomach for the guys to fight over which one has dibs on the red head. "I see you! I'm coming out."

I take the steps two at a time and shove open the bus door. Aubrey spots me immediately and pushes past security to grab me up in a tight hug. "I've been waiting for freaking ever." She releases me and shoves her auburn curls over her shoulder. "It's good to see you too. I've missed you."

I grab her hand. "Come on. I want you to meet the guys before they all take off on their two day reprieve."

Aubrey giggles with excitement and allows me to pull her onto the bus. All three guys immediately stop talking when we step inside and turn toward us. The curiosity burns in their eyes as I pull Aubrey beside me. "Guys, this is my closest friend, Aubrey. Aubrey this is Black Falcon. This is Trip"—I point to him—"he's the drummer. And this is his twin brother, Tyke—also the bass player. And last but not least—"

"Riff." He takes a step and shakes Aubrey's hand as he introduces himself.

His eyes glue to hers and she giggles again. I have never seen her so unhitched and nervous. Both of her cheeks are turning pink as they shake hands for an extra lengthy time period. The twins seem to notice it too. Trip slaps Riff on the back. "Later man." Then he and Tyke go out to round up other girls.

I clear my throat, and Aubrey lets go of Riff's hand. "So, um, Aubrey, what do you want to do today?"

She finally pulls her eyes away from Riff and says, "Doesn't matter."

"How about we all hang out," Riff says.

Heavy boots clomp onto the kitchen floor. Noel's showered and looking down right sexy in tight jeans and black t-shirt. The material clings to his chest and shows off his body perfectly. I bite my lip, and Aubrey elbows me.

Damn. I glance away quickly and hook some loose hair behind my ear. Heat creeps up my neck and I can't make myself look at her. I know, without a doubt, she's got that smug I-know-you-like-him look on her face.

"What's going on?" Noel asks as he grabs a bottle of water from the refrigerator.

"Noel this is my friend, Aubrey. The one I was telling you about."

He gives her a nod and then points his attention to Riff, who hasn't taken his eyes off my friend since she set foot on this bus. "You're going out with these two?"

Riff blinks hard a couple times, like he's breaking out of trance. "Yeah, I mean, if they are cool with that."

Before I can object, Aubrey says, "Absolutely."

Riff grins at her again and then puts on his sunglasses while he heads for the bus door. "Awesome. Let's get this show on the road."

I grab Aubrey's arm before she follows him out like a little puppy. "What the hell are you doing?"

She shrugs. "He's hot and seems into me. What's the problem?"

There really isn't one. I just don't want her to get crushed by an asshole like Riff. "Nothing, I guess. Just be cautious. I don't want to see you get hurt."

Aubrey leans in and kisses my cheek. "I'm a big girl, Lanie. I'm just here to have a good time, not get married. I know what I'm doing."

I throw my arms around her neck and hug her. "Of course, have a good time."

She grins before she follows Riff out the door. I watch through the bus window as she meets up with him, and he holds out his hand to her like they've known each other for years and head towards the Escalade.

"Huh? Well that was unexpected," Noel says and then gulps down the rest of his water.

"Tell me about it."

The four of us pile into the SUV and go to dinner at a local Mexican restaurant. Riff and Aubrey sit next to each other, a little too close for my liking, the entire time. Noel seems unfazed to the new pair as he sits back in the booth with his arms stretched out along the back. We fall into easy conversation, telling Riff and Aubrey stories about some of the fun we had when were in school together.

"Sounds like you two were quite the pair back then," Aubrey says after a sip of her margarita.

I smile at Noel. "Yeah, we were great friends back in the day."

Noel cocks his head to the side and gazes down at me with his blue eyes. "Friend, huh? Ouch. That's all I was to you?"

I smack his shoulder, not hard enough to really hurt, though. "You know what I mean."

"Damn." He rubs his right bicep and then leans his back against the booth. "See you still pack a hell of a punch. Haven't seen you throw a shot like that since the time you fought Jessica Cranbee over a Barbie doll back in fourth grade. Remember that?"

I laugh as I rest my elbows on the table and take a drink of my Margarita. "Yeah. That girl was always such a bitch, wasn't she?"

"She was." He bumps my shoulder with his. "But she never messed with you again after that. I think you were the only girl in our class she didn't scare the shit out of."

I smile at Noel. "Yeah, I don't get that. Why people have to be mean." The words are practically my size seven shoes shoved square in my mouth. Who am I to talk about being mean to people? Maybe it's not the right time to bring this up, but after six of these margaritas I can't stop myself from saying, "Look, Noel, the way we ended things...I'm sorry."

He reaches out and takes a strand of my brown hair between his fingers and twirls it. "Water under the bridge, Lane. Let's not ruin a perfect night with something we can't change."

By the time we're on our eighth round of margaritas, I'm feeling pretty good, even my toes are tingling. We don't bring up the topic of our break-up anymore. We just continue to drink and tell funny stories. The tension between Noel and Riff even seems lighter for some reason, too.

After we finish gorging ourselves with drinks and food, Noel pays the bill. Once I'm standing outside, the liquor hits hard. I stumble in the parking lot as we head towards the SUV.

Noel wraps his arms around me and pulls me against him so I don't topple over. "Easy there, lightweight. You alright?"

This time I embrace the closeness between us and throw my arms around his waist. "I'm good. Just starting to feel a little tired…and drunk."

Noel chuckles. "That's what happens when you stand up after hammering, what, nine margaritas? Shit hits you fast."

I shake my head. "Eight," I correct.

Aubrey and Riff slide into the middle row together, which means Noel and I have to share a seat. Mike shuts us inside and I giggle as Noel and I climb into the third row. "Does he always go everywhere with you?"

"Who? Mike?"

I nod, and my head suddenly feels very heavy and Noel's shoulder beside me looks awfully comfortable. It's crossing the line, but so is drinking to the point of intoxication with a business client. The conscious part of my brain screams at me not to do it, but the drunken tired side of me tells me to go for it. I curl into him and lay my head half on his chest and shoulder.

He sighs contently and wraps his arm around me, while resting his cheek on the top of my head.

It actually feels pretty nice wrapped in his embrace again.

He strokes my hair a couple times, and I close my eyes at the softness of his touch. "Yeah, I suppose he does. Mike's a good guy. Maybe even my best friend. We spend a lot of time together."

I snuggle in tighter and lay my arm across his lap. "That's nice."

I'm completely comfortable lying against Noel's toned chest. It's probably the margaritas talking, but I feel the urge to kiss him. We've had such a good time all night. It almost feels like the right thing to do because I want him to know how much fun I had with this sweet version of him. Physical show of emotion was the only thing Noel every really understood clearly.

I sigh and try to block out the thought. We aren't kids anymore. Kissing him while I'm tipsy will lead to other things. I know my body well enough that when it comes to Noel Falcon, it has a hard time resisting his touch.

Aubrey and Riff lean into each other and kiss right in front of us. Noel's fingers stop running through my hair and slide down my back. They stop at the hem of shirt and trace the skin on the small of my back. My breath catches, and his chest moves a little quicker. Seeing something so intimate while so close to him causes a fire to ignite in my stomach.

I bring my hand up to the neck of his shirt and run my finger along the exposed flesh right above it. Fingers on my back slip inside the waist band of my jeans, and his other hand finds my chin and tips it up towards him. Noels hooded eyes stare into mine, and something in me stirs. For the first time since being here, I think about giving into his attempt to kiss me. His thumb traces my bottom lip, and I close my eyes.

Noel leans into me and presses his lips to my forehead.

I slump against him a little, and he chuckles before he whispers, "I want to kiss you, but I know once I start, I won't be able to control myself."

I swallow, knowing he's right, and in this perfect moment, I think I just might let him do all the things he's been threatening to do to my body.

I start to pull away, but Noel doesn't loosen his hold. I turn my head and watch my friend make-out with the rock star in front of me. I sure hope she knows what she's doing.

We arrive back at the bus and all I can think about is going to bed and getting some distance between Noel and I before things get out of hand. Liquor still courses through my veins, and I know I won't make proper judgment calls around him. I trudge back into the bedroom and search for a t-shirt to change into.

Aubrey follows me into the room. "Aren't you going over to the hotel with the rest of the band?"

I shake my head. "I can't afford a room over there, and I'm tired. All I can think about is sleeping."

She studies me. "Sleeping? After the way you were flirting with Noel tonight, you want to go to sleep?"

I shrug and pretend that Noel and I didn't just have a moment in the backseat. "Yes? What's so wrong with that?"

She bites her lip. "You two have this whole connection thing vibing between you. Aren't you the least big curious as to what it can turn into?"

"No. This is business, Aubrey. It can't be anything more than that between us. You know that."

She hugs me. "I love you, Lanie, but some times you need to loosen up and say fuck the rules. A job isn't everything. Live a little, you know."

I laugh and try to divert her attention off me. "Like you are with Riff?"

Aubrey blushes. "I can't help it. I've always thought he was the cutest in this band. Gah! He's a really good kisser, too."

I plug my ears. "I so don't need to hear these details."

She pulls my hands down and laughs. "Trust me, by this time tomorrow I'll have more details about Riff than how he kisses."

I smack her arm. "Go then, and slut around, if you must."

She winks at me. "Oh, that's a definite must."

I roll my eyes as she darts out the door and into what will be a night she'll brag about for months.

Great.

I change as quickly as I can and turn to get into bed just as Noel opens the door without knocking. I scowl at him for the intrusion. "I could've been naked."

He grins. "I was sort of hoping for that."

"Men," I grumble as I slide into the bed.

He chuckles as he closes the door behind him and pulls off his shirt. I turn my back to him to give him some privacy to change. The springs groan as he gets into bed next to me and shuts off the lights.

"Aren't you going to the hotel tonight?"

"Wasn't planning on it. Besides I was kind of hoping you wanted to cuddle with me some more."

I roll over and face him. Even in the dark, his magnetism doesn't escape me. I fight the urge to trace my fingertips along his stubbly jaw to find out what it feels like. If I did that, it'd be all over. The boundaries I've established with him will go right out the window, yet, I can't force myself to turn away.

The energy flowing between us, in this small, dark room, is powerful. I bite my bottom lip, practically tasting the lust in the air. Noel reaches up and caresses my cheek with his thumb. I should tell him to stop, but the fire in his touch makes my body crave more of his skin on mine. His eyes roam over me. I study every inch of his face. It's so beautiful. The look in his eyes shows hope, but I'm not sure sleeping with him is a good choice. I can't let him think I'm like all of his random groupies. I want more from him than causal sex. Which sounds completely selfish considering I'm the one who left him before—I really have no right to demand anything of him.

"Lane." The way he says my name makes my toes curl. "I'm still crazy over you. I know it's been a while, but it feels like just yesterday when you walked out of my life. When you left me, I was so empty. There was this huge, gaping hole in my heart that no one could fill. I tried to get over you. I really did, but you were always there. Every woman I kissed was you."

My heart clenches at his words. He's pretty much laid all his cards out for me to see. I'll admit there is something between us, and it's strong, but at this point I'm not sure if it's just purely a sexual thing. And I can't chance my career on such a crazy risk.

I sigh. We can't rush this.

"Noel, we have to stay professional. I work for you now—how's it going to look if I sleep with you my first week here. Who'll take me serious? Diana encourages me to do whatever it takes to keep you happy, but I'm afraid if I sleep with you, we'll step over a line we shouldn't, at least while I work for you, anyway."

He leans in closer, his lips just inches from my face. "So quit. I'll take care of you. You don't need to work as long as you're with me. I'll take care of everything you need."

"You don't get it—still after all this time. This job is my dream, Noel. If I sleep with you now and things go bad, not only will I lose you, but my dream as well."

He frowns. "This project means that much to you? It isn't just about getting close to me?"

I shake my head and then pull his fingers away from my face and lace mine with his. "No. I mean, at first it was just the job, but now, after this, I can't kid myself. There's still something between us…"

"But?" he prompts.

"We can't act on it. Things have to go slow, maybe after Diana sees I can actually do this, she'll take me serious. Once that happens, maybe we can give us a shot."

Noel traces my lips with his finger. "I don't think I can live without at least kissing these. How about we make another deal?"

I tilt my head. Noel always has some sort of scheme brewing in that devilish mind of his. Before he has a chance to set the terms, I come up with some of my own that I can live with while still getting this project done. "How about for every kiss I give you, I get ten minutes of uninterrupted time working on the charity project."

Noel smiles up at me through sexy, long lashes. "Sure, I'll agree to that. But I warn you, if you kiss me like you mean it too much, I won't promise to hold off."

A fierce blush spreads all over my face.

"How about we start with one right now?"

Before I can answer, Noel pulls my lips to his. The warmth of his mouth is so familiar. I close my eyes and shut my brain off. Nothing else matters but the here and now. This kiss—the one I've been reliving in my mind over the past few years—is finally happening.

My lips part, and his tongue finds mine, swirling around like a well-practiced routine. A sound of intense need catches in the back of his throat, and I press my body against his.

His hand slips under my shirt and brushes against the skin on the small of my back. I shiver. The feel of his skin on me floods me with desire. I can't remember ever wanting Noel as badly as I do now. Maybe it's because I know what I've been missing. Or maybe it's because he's turned into an incredibly attractive man. Either way, he's the only thing I want in the world right now, and I can't get close enough to him.

My hand flies into Noel's hair as he slides his hand down the length of my body. His fingers dig into my thighs before he hitches my leg around his hip. He pushes his pelvis into mine and all that separates us is a couple of thin pieces of fabric. His erection strains against his boxers—Noel wants this just as much as I do.

He trails kisses across my jaw. I toss my head back and arch my chest into him. "Oh God, Lane. You smell fucking amazing." A shudder rips through his body as I moan in his ear.

The sound of my own voice catches me off guard. I rise up. All I can focus on is his blue eyes, alive with intense need. He wants me to say I need him—that I want him to take me. Here and now. But I can't do that. We have to slow down.

I push him back a little. "Wait a second. We agreed to only kiss."

"You can't kiss me like that and not expect me to get turned on."

I turn away from him and blush.

Noel pulls my face toward him. "Don't," he whispers, "don't be ashamed. It's incredibly sexy when you let yourself go like that. I never knew you had that in you."

"People can change. I have grown up a little. I'm not that same silly, naïve girl you knew back in high school."

He grins. "Well, I liked her, too, you know. But this version of you is down right fuckable."

My face heats up and I roll away from him. Noel sits up and pushes himself off the bed before grabbing his shirt from the floor.

"Where are you going?"

He grabs a towel out of one of the drawers. "To take a cold shower—I have a feeling I'll need a lot of those these next two weeks if we keep kissing like that."

I flop back onto the bed when Noel shuts the door behind him. He has no clue the same goes for me.

Chapter 12

The next morning I wake up before Noel and creep out of the bedroom with my cell in hand, doing my best not to wake him. I dial Aubrey's number and then look at the clock. It's only a little after eight. She's going to kill me for waking her up, but I have to know that she got back to her hotel okay.

She answers on the fourth ring. "Hello?" Her tone is raspy and slow.

"I'm sorry I didn't mean to wake you, but I wanted to know what your plans are for today."

She giggles. "Stop, Riff."

I roll my eyes. "You're still with him?"

"Yes," she says, breathlessly.

I frown, knowing she's probably going to spend the rest of her time here with Riff. "So I take it you're busy."

Aubrey sighs. "Don't be mad. We'll be together all the time in about a week when you come home. Besides you have Noel to play with."

"You know it's not like that."

She giggles again. "But it could be *just* like that if you'd let it." Riff mumbles something in the background and I hear the distinct sound of sucking. "Um, gotta go, Lanie. Love you."

Before I can get another word of protest in, she hangs up. Aubrey's always been one to live a little on the wild side. I guess, her messing around with Riff should've been expected. He's a horn ball and she has a thing for the bad-boy type. I should've seen that one coming.

I lay my phone on the table and run my fingers through my hair. A strong pair of tattooed arms wraps around my waist, and I stiffen. "Noel, what are you doing?"

He pulls the hair away from my neck and kisses the delicate skin there. "I thought we made our feelings for each other pretty clear last night."

I pull away from him. "Just because I said I feel something for you, doesn't mean we get to act on it."

Noel scratches the back of his neck. "I don't get you, Lane. One minute your hot for me, the next you shove me away. Aren't I more important than some lame job?"

"Noel…"

He shakes his head. "You know what, forget it. Sorry I crossed some invisible line you have drawn in your head."

I watch him stalk off towards the bedroom and slam the door.

A few hours later, when Aubrey and Riff are forced out of their sex nest, I stand back stage with her while we wait on the guys to come out of their band meeting. She grins from ear to ear as she goes over every sordid detail of her sexual escapade last night. I roll my eyes at the part where she gushes about how great Riff is in the sack, and she gives me a playful shove.

"So you're telling me nothing happened with you and Noel last night?" she questions. "You two were pretty cozy on the way back." I sigh, and she laughs. "I knew it! Tell me!"

I hold my hands up in surrender. "Okay. Okay. Jeesh, get a grip. We kissed."

Aubrey raises her eyebrow. "A kiss? Was it like a polite peck or was it full on tongue I-want-your-body make-out?"

I frown. "It definitely wasn't polite."

"Lanie, God, sometimes I swear for someone so smart, you sometimes act like an idiot. You should be ecstatic right now. Reconnection with your first love is something people dream about and you're getting that. I don't see why you don't just let loose and let it happen."

"But the job—"

"But, *nothing*. Don't make me give the 'jobs aren't everything' speech. Jobs don't keep you warm or make you feel sexy, but Noel Falcon totally can. Anyone can see the guy is crazy about you."

Is it really that obvious to other people? I know he's been trying to get in my pants since we meet back up in Houston, but it wasn't until last night I found out he has actual feelings for me, and that scares me a little. It's obvious I hurt him in the past, and I don't want to do that again. Things are going smooth between us now, but what happens when my two weeks are up? Will he go back to sleeping with random groupies while I'm back in New York? If he did that, I would end our relationship…again.

Then there's the job.

I don't think I'm ready to risk anything just yet.

Aubrey stares at me expectantly. "Quit doing that."

I flinch. "Doing what?"

"Over thinking things. You'll never know until you let down your walls a little."

I run my fingers through my hair. "Why are you pushing this? You hated him before."

She shrugs. "Because you're my best friend, and I love you. I want you to be happy. Plus, he's not the asshole I thought he was."

I give her a weak smile and then wrap my arms around her.

"Hey now…" I turn and find Riff staring at us. "Nobody gets this girl's lovin' but me."

Aubrey giggles like a giddy kid at Christmas when Riff grabs her up in a hug. "Riff!"

I roll my eyes. "On that note, I'm out of here."

I wander around back stage and find an empty bench. The roadies rush back and forth connecting cables and tuning instruments. The opening act for Black Falcon is set to take the stage in the next few minutes. I'm really enjoying all the great music I've heard the last couple shows and I'm curious as to what band is playing with them tonight.

"Lanie, love, didn't expect to see you again so soon." I jerk my head towards the voice and set my eyes on a grinning Striker. His long, dark hair hangs in a low ponytail and a few shorter strands fall haphazardly around his face. The brown in his eyes is so dark they almost appear black from a short distance. Tight leather pants accompanied with a sleeveless dress shirt shows off his body and array of perfectly placed tattoos. I'm definitely intrigued by him.

I smile at him. "Hey, Striker. I didn't know Embrace the Darkness was opening for Black Falcon."

Striker must take my smile as an invitation because he plops down next to me on the bench and causally stretches his arm behind me. "We do from time to time. Same record label and all. Say, you think you might fancy getting a drink with me later?"

When I gave my number to him the other day, I didn't even think about the possibility of something happening between Noel and I. But, since we kissed last night, I feel like that changes things a bit.

"Striker, I'm not sure…"

"Ah, come on. Just one drink." He winks at me, and when I hesitate with my answer, he says, "Don't tell me you've got a thing going on with that Noel, bloke. He's not worthy of a lovely such as you."

I raise an eyebrow, taken back at his forwardness. "And you are?"

Striker takes my hand into his and then raises it to his lips. "I would treat you like the queen you are."

The skin on the back of my hand tingles from the touch of his lips. His eyes meet mine, and there is no trace of humor in them at all. I swallow deeply, unsure of what to say. Noel and I've already had a relationship that's fallen apart. Who says that won't happen again? This thing with Striker is new and unexplored, and frankly a little scary because our apparent attraction to one another feels intense.

"What the hell is going on?" Noel's face is angry, and he's staring daggers at my hand in Striker's.

I yank my hand away, and my heart pounds. Where did he come from? "Nothing. It's not what you think."

Striker stares at me and tilts his head. There's an emotion of recognition on his face, like his suspicions of Noel and me is confirmed. "Pity."

I open my mouth to apologize, but I shut it quickly. There really isn't anything to say I'm sorry for. I don't really know Striker. I shouldn't have to explain my relationship with Noel to him when I'm still trying to figure it out myself.

After a few seconds, Striker sighs roughly before standing to face Noel. "This one's a good girl, mate. Treat her right."

Noel doesn't answer, just narrows his eyes as he watches Striker walk away, and then turns his attention back to me. "What the hell was that?"

"He was just being nice," I counter.

"Nice? Kissing your fucking hand is crossing the damn line," he growls.

I stand and shove my hands on my hips. "*Nothing* happened!"

He jams his fingers into his hair. "You're driving me insane. I can't keep doing this, Lane."

I stare at him with my mouth open slightly. "Noel..."

"Just stop." He closes his eyes. "Just stop, okay. You're ripping my heart out and you don't even know it."

"I'm sorry, I just need more time. We don't have to rush things."

He grabs me in his arms. "Yes we do. If I don't have you soon, I'm going to implode. Can't you see that? I want you to be with me. I can't stand all these guys coming on to you. The fact that I'm not allowed to do a God damn thing about it because you're not mine is killing me."

My heart thumps against my ribs as he holds me tight against his chest. I dip my head down and close my eyes. "I'm sorry. I don't mean to hurt you, I just..."

Just what? Don't love him? Don't want him? I can't say that because it would be a lie. I lean my head into his chest and sigh. Aubrey's right. Noel is crazy about me. More than anything right now I want to tell him how I feel, but I know if I do everything will change.

Am I ready for that?

"Just what, Lane?" his voice rumbles in his chest. "Tell me what you want."

"I can't," I whisper.

Noel sighs then pulls away. I gaze up at him, and he closes his eyes. When he steps back, I grab for his hand, desperate to keep him close, but he moves too quick.

He turns away, and there's a tug in my heart towards him.

"Wait..." I say, and he stops in his tracks.

"For what? To be led on some more?" he asks with his back still towards me.

When I don't reply, he shoves his hands in his jean pockets and storms off. Tears blur my vision and I watch him until he disappears around a corner. Why can't I just bring myself to say fuck the job and go for Noel? I can see how much I'm hurting him, and it can all be fixed if I just tell him I want him, too.

Chapter 13

I check my cell phone. The eighth text to Noel since his set ended still goes unanswered. He knows I wanted to leave for my parent's house as soon as the show was over. No doubt he's pissed at me for missing the performance, but seeing him so soon after our fight would've been too much. I needed to get my head clear and think about what's important to me.

The last text I send says, I'm leaving without him.

I sigh and grab my overnight bag and step into the night air. Guess I'm going solo. I hop into the red Jetta we rented earlier to make the trip and toss my stuff on the passenger seat. Everything is such a mess, and I don't understand how it even got this way.

Thirty minutes into my drive, I pull through an all night drive-thru and sit in the parking lot to eat. My eating habits as of late have been less than stellar, so it feels good to eat a carb induced meal.

When I'm about fifteen minutes out from my parent's house, I call my mom. "Hey, can you leave the door unlocked for me. I'll be there soon."

I glance at the clock on the dash. It's well after midnight.

"Okay, sweetheart. I'll try to wait up for you."

I smile and tell her I love her.

Right after I end the call, my cell chirps with a text message. My heart stops for a split second as I read Noel's words.

Meet me on the dock.

He's there, waiting on me. Emotions flood me, and I don't realize I'm speeding like a bat out of hell until I glance down at the speedometer. I take a deep breath and try to mentally prepare myself for what I'm going to say to him.

The minute I pull into my parent's driveway, I exit the car and head down to the dock. It's really dark out here. I could kick myself for not grabbing the flashlight from the house first, but I'm almost through the wooded area behind my childhood home—it doesn't make sense to turn back now. I'm too close.

The clock on my cell flashes 12:45am, and I sigh. This is crazy. I can't believe he came, not to mention he's waiting at our special spot. When he didn't answer me earlier, I figured he was out licking shots off a groupie's stomach or something equally as wild.

Insecurity is one of my biggest downfalls and I know it. It's the main reason I ended things with Noel. I wanted a secure future, not to struggle day in and day out.

Two steps later I'm at the top of the hill on a path leading down to the lake. The moonlight bounces off the ripples on the water. I forgot how beautiful it is after dark. My eyes strain down at the dock, and they instantly widen.

There he is, sitting on the railing with his elbows resting on his knees.

He turns his head toward me, and my heart stops. Noel is breathtaking by the light of the moon. This feels very intimate and very familiar. I know once I go down there, I'll be a goner.

That last thought makes me want to turn and run back to my car as quick as I can, but, instead, I lift my chin high and force my feet forward, ready to figure this thing out between us.

Noel stands when my shoes hit the wooden dock. His perfect face stretches into a lazy grin as I near. My heart speeds up a notch, and I bite the inside of my cheek. He actually looks happy to see me, which takes me back. I thought he was pissed at me for all the mixed signals.

I lift my hand in a wave.

"What's this waving shit?" He rushes over and grabs me around the waist and hoists me off the ground.

The laugh that bubbles out of my throat surprises me as he spins me around. I was prepared for another fight. How weird is it that we can hug and laugh like there isn't bad blood between us? I squeeze my arms around his neck and inhale his manly scent as I melt into his muscled chest.

"Noel," I squeal and a thrill shoots through me as I say his name. "I'll be sick."

That only makes him laugh harder as he stops spinning and sets me to my feet. His hand cups my cheek. "God, Lane. I'm an idiot. I'm sorry."

I sigh audibly, and instantly I wish I could just curl up in a ball and die from pure embarrassment. I can't believe I actually swooned a little just now. I try to drop out of his gaze, but his hand holds me steady as he waits for me to say something. Noel raises an eyebrow. "Is it okay that I'm here? You don't hate me?"

Oh my God. Hate him? I think about Noel like a love-sick puppy, but there's no way in hell I'm telling him that. How pathetic would that make me if he thinks I've sat around all evening pinning for him? So, instead, I smile and say, "I could never hate you."

He tucks some hair behind my ear. "Good because that would kill me. I'm sorry I tried to rush you. Relationships take time. I get that. It's just I want you so much. I don't think clearly when it comes to you. So, I'm sorry. I'll try and slow down."

Still locked in his arms, my fingers itch to touch his face. "I'm sorry, too."

Noel cocks his head to the side and gazes down at me with his blue eyes. "You know, I understand where you were coming from when you left me last time we were here. Hell, even I'm surprised I made it in this biz. You were always the level headed one." He smiles and looks into my eyes. "But I'm sorry for that, too—for the way things turned out. I should've gone after you—made things right between us. That we could still work. I didn't know that's how you felt about me, and it killed me. I didn't even know how to fix us after that."

I shook my head. "It wasn't totally your fault, Noel. Things were all changing so fast—high school was ending and becoming an adult scared me. I wanted you to come to school with me—to still be with me. I was being selfish. I shouldn't have been so pushy. I knew who you were and I shouldn't have tried to change your dream. It was wrong of me, and I'm sorry." I let out a huge sigh. "I've wanted to tell you that for so long, but I figured since you never spoke to me again after that night out here on the dock, that you hated my guts."

The corners of his lips turn down and his fingertips trace my cheek. "I could never hate you, either. I loved you."

A tear slips from my eye at the sound of his words. A million pounds fly off my heart. He doesn't hate me. "Thank you," I whisper.

Noel brushes my eye with his thumb and then cradles my face in both hands. A smile flirts along his lips. My heart thunders with anticipation of a kiss, and I bite my lip.

Noel's eyes search my face. "Can I kiss you?"

I close my eyes and bite my lip. He has no clue how much I want to feel his lips on mine again. Every cell in my body quivers with need for this man, and it scares me a little to know he has this effect on me. It'll be easy for my heart to crumble if this doesn't work out.

I shake the last thought out of my head, and Noel frowns. "Is that a no?" I panic a little because I don't want him to think I'm rejecting him again. This calls for immediate action.

I wrap my arms around his neck and pull my body against his. "Definitely not a no."

That's all it takes.

Noel crushes his mouth to mine. The warmth spreads clear down to my toes as I melt into him. My lips part, and his tongue finds mine, slowly massaging. A sound catches in the back of his throat as I grip two handfuls of his hair in my fists and push my body against his.

Noel's hand slides under my shirt and his fingers trail along the skin on the small of my back. I shiver. Heat spreads through me and I find myself breathing hard.

Noel grips both of my hips and then glides his touch down my legs. His fingers dig into my thighs as he hoists me up onto the rail. My knees open, and he pushes between them. His erection strains against his jeans as he grinds into me.

He trails kisses down my neck and I toss my head back, arching my chest into him.

"Oh God, Lane. I want you so fucking much." A shudder tears through him as I moan in his ear.

He grabs my chin between his forefinger and thumb. Blue eyes, alive with intense need, stare at me. He kisses my lips, and I close my eyes. He wants my permission to take it to the next level. All I have to do is say the words and he'll heal this aching need inside of me.

I lean in and trace his top lip with my tongue. "I've missed you," I whispered.

Noel's mouth takes mine—our kisses deep and frenzied. I wrap my legs around his waist and grind my pelvis into his. The wood rail is rough against my butt through my jeans. He pulls back and sucks in a quick breath through his teeth. "Are you sure?"

His forehead rests against mine. The need to kiss him some more is overwhelming. I smile and yank his face back to me.

Noel grabs the hem of his black t-shirt and yanks it over his head. He tosses it on the dock. His bare chest is a wondrous sight to behold. The tips of my fingers glide down his pecs and stop to linger on his well defined abs.

Noel quirks his right, pierced eyebrow and wears the most devilish smile I've ever seen. "You like those, huh?"

My tongue darts out, wetting my lips before I chew on my bottom one. Of course I like it. What red-blooded woman wouldn't? He's damn near perfect. I was out of my mind when I walked out on him before.

His lips claim mine, and his tattooed arms pull me in tight. Noel lets out a growl in my mouth, and it's unbelievably sexy to know I caused it to happen. I grab the waistband of his jeans and pop open the button. He groans as I slowly unzip them and reach inside. "No underwear?"

He shakes his head and then traces my top lip with his tongue. "They always seem to get in the way."

I giggle as he kisses my throat. "Uh-huh? You mean like right now?" I wrap my fingers around the base of him and give a tight squeeze.

He sucks in air through his teeth. "Jesus. Exactly like right now."

I withdraw my hand from his jeans and lick my fingers and the palm of my hand. Noels eyes widen. "Since when did you get so kinky?"

I shrug. "Since when did you decide underwear was a bad thing?"

I shove my hand back inside his jean and begin to stroke his considerable length. He gasps. "Point taken."

His flesh is warm and solid in my hand. My hand barely wraps around it he's so big.

My pace increases, and Noel's breathing grows steady in my ear. He wraps his long fingers around my wrist. "I'm already too damn excited. If you keep that up, I won't be able to hold back much longer." I slow my motion down, and he kisses my lips. "That's it, baby. I wanna make this last. No need to rush."

His words send a thrill through every inch of me. I can't believe I'm this turned on already. The moisture in my panties presses against my skin. Noel's hand slides under my shirt and trails its way up to my breast. All I can think about is him touching me.

"It's been so long since I've been with anybody real," he says between kisses.

That statement makes me wonder just how many non-real people he's been with. He is a rock star for God's sake. The numbers are probably well into the hundreds.

My stomach turns a little at the thought of these lips all over tons of different women, and I fight back the urge to throw him off of me based on the principal alone. Sleeping with him tonight wasn't my intention when I came out here. I figured we'd talk—figure things out. Instead, we'd barely talked five minutes before we'd gone straight into sex like we used to after a fight in this exact same spot.

"Noel…" His name slips out of my mouth almost like a moan. I meant it to come out stern so he would get the point maybe this wasn't a good idea until we talked a little, but it totally didn't sound that way. It sounded encouraging, like my body is enjoying his touch too much to turn him away.

I open my mouth to tell him to slow down, and right on cue my cell phone rings in my pocket. *"Your mother is calling. Answer your phone. I'll just keep calling."*

Noel laughs at my stupid ring tone for my mom as I reach in my pocket and hit ignore.

He sweeps my hair away from my neck and trails his nose against my skin. "Mmmmm, I'm tempted to just eat you right here."

"Noel—"

"Your mother is calling. Answer your phone. I'll just keep calling." I roll my eyes and hit ignore again.

Noel rests his forehead against mine. "Maybe you should call her back. Could be important."

I sigh and pull the phone out of my pocket. *Mothers.*

Mom answers on the first ring. "Lanie? Where are you? Are you all right?"

I roll my eyes again. "Calm down, Mom. I'm fine. Really."

Noel snuggles against me and kisses my cheek while I explain to Mom that I am out on the boat dock with Noel.

She sighs with relief. "Thank God you're alright. I saw your car in the driveway and knew you hadn't come in the house and started to panic. There are some real crazies out there, you know. You scared me to death."

"Well, don't worry. I'm perfectly fine. We'll be there in a couple of minutes," I say just before I tell her goodbye and hang up.

Noel's lip pokes out a little, and he gives me puppy dog eyes. "You're going to leave me like this?"

I place a hand on his chest. "I'm sorry, Noel. This just feels really fast, plus this whole job thing is still going on."

His thumb caresses by cheek, and his eyes roam over me. I study every inch of his face. It's so beautiful, and the sad look in his eyes will haunt me for the rest of my life. This rejection is not the best way to end our reunion, but I'm not sure sleeping with him is any better of a choice. I can't let him think I'm like all of his random groupies.

"Lane." The way he says my name makes my toes curl. "I'm still crazy over you." He runs his hand through his hair. "What I'm trying to say is…I'm sorry. I just got ahead of myself here. You seemed so into it." He drops his hands to his sides, and he looks into my eyes. "I just want you back."

Noel backs away from me and grabs his shirt from the rail. The cold air rushes over my skin when he shoves his hands in his pockets after covering his chest with his shirt. He shrugs and turns to walk away from me. I swallow hard as I watch him make his way down the dock. My hand clutches my chest and tears blur my vision. Is this how he felt when I left him standing here four years ago? A lost and broken shell.

I can't let this happen. I've been miserable without him, and he just confessed he felt the same way. This is stupid. Two people who love each other so much should be able to work through anything.

My legs wobble beneath me as I hop off the rail. Noel is halfway up the hill already so I kick off my flip-flops and sprint down the dock—the wood rough beneath my feet. "Noel!" My voice breaks a little as I call his name. He turns just in time to open his arms and catch me as I fling myself into his arms. "Don't leave. Please."

His arms circle my waist, and he buries his face in my long, brown hair. "I wasn't going anywhere—only giving you some space. I'll do anything you want to make this happen between us, including give you time because I can't lose you again. It hurts too fucking much."

A surge of bravery shoots through me, and I kiss his lips.

Chapter 14

The next morning the smell of bacon and eggs wake me. I roll over and stare around my childhood room. A picture of Noel and I at prom together sits on my night stand. I trace my fingers over his face and warmth spreads all through me. It feels good to reconnect with him, like a part of me that was missing is back again.

Once I clear the bottom step, I see Noel in the kitchen with my mother. She looks so tiny next to him as she teaches him how to flip a pancake. Noel's dark hair sticks up in every direction, and his blue eyes focus on the task in front of him. Mom laughs as Noel flips the pancake outside the pan.

I smile. It's nice to see they still get along so well.

Noel notices me leaning against the wall watching him and he grins. "Hey, you! I was attempting to make you breakfast in bed, but I'm kind of screwing it up."

My mom pats him on the shoulder. "Honey, you're doing a great job. It just takes a little practice and finesse."

I giggle when Noel flips another, and it slides half-way across the pan. Guess he's not perfect at everything he does. It's nice to see him back in a normal environment without all the rock star glam. Reminds me of the guy I loved in the first place.

I walk over and stand beside him at the stove. "Can I help?"

Mom unties her apron and hands it to me. "I'm going for a little walk. You two enjoy breakfast."

I take the apron from her, and she pats my cheek. It's good to see her smile. She hasn't done that much since Dad died. Her cheeks are a rosy-pink, and she's looking more like her old self. People say I look just like her with my dark hair and green eyes, but I know I'm no beauty like her. She has beautiful fair skin, while mine has more of an olive tint to it like my dad.

When my mother is gone, I turn back to Noel. He places two plates of pancakes on the kitchen table and then pulls out a chair for me.

"It looks great." I can't believe he put so much effort into this as I notice the bacon and eggs on the table. "You didn't have to go to all the trouble though. I would've been good with cereal."

He laughs as he sits down beside me. "Are you kidding? I'm not going to turn down an offer from Kathy to learn how to cook. Her food is always amazing."

I smile at the warm compliant about Mom. "She always did like you—she and dad both."

Noel stops cutting his pancakes, and he frowns. "Why didn't you tell me about your dad?"

I shrug and pour syrup on my plate to distract myself from crying. "Never really came up. Plus it's easier if I don't think about it too much."

He takes my hand into his. "You should've told me he died. I would've been there for you. I'm so sorry. I really liked Jim."

I squeeze his hand. "Thank you. It was so unexpected, you know. Who would have thought he would have gotten diagnosised with cancer at forty-nine? He went pretty quickly, so he didn't suffer much. But it was still hard—the first year without him especially. "

"I wish I could've been there for you."

I touch his cheek. The stubble prickles my fingertips. "But you're here now."

He pulls my hand to his lips and kisses my fingers. "And I'm never going anywhere again."

After we wash up all the dishes, we go out to the garage in search of some fishing gear. Noel sorts through all the poles until he comes to the bright pink one I always used when we used to go.

He hands it to me. "I remember this old thing."

I laugh and take it from him, and he turns to pick one out for himself. "You remember it because this girlie thing always out fishes you."

He grabs the tackle box and rolls his eyes. "Come on, Ms. Fisherman. Show me how it's done, then."

It's amazingly easy being with Noel now. The tension between not knowing how to approach one another is gone. While I'm still not completely sure how a relationship between Noel and I will affect my job, at this point it doesn't seem that important. Only being with him does.

I sigh as we step on the dock. This place holds so many great memories, not only of Noel and I, but days spent with my father, too.

Noel sits our stuff down and wraps his arms around me. I lean into him, glad to feel his warmth and comfort around me. The spicy cologne on his chest is delicious and a welcome distraction to the emotion going on in my brain.

He pulls back and gives me a quick peck. "Ready to do this?"

I raise an eyebrow. "Only if you are ready to have your ass handed to you by a girl."

He chuckles and gives me another quick kiss before going to work baiting our hooks with fake worms. We spend the rest of the afternoon on the dock talking and fishing. I've missed this—being with Noel.

Close to three o'clock we pack everything up so we can get cleaned up before dinner. Noel takes my hand into his as we walk back to the house, and he grins as I thread my fingers through his.

When we make it to the top of the hill, I notice Mom setting up the back patio for dinner.

"Anything we can help you with?" Noel asks.

Mom smiles as she takes in the sight of our hands locked together. "Nope. I actually have everything under control. I did forget dessert though, so I'm going to run over to the market and pick up an apple pie and maybe some wine. The steaks are marinating and we'll throw them on the grill when I come back."

Noel nods and takes the fishing gear back to the garage for us.

"Okay, then. I'm going to take a quick shower and get ready," I tell her as I follow her into the house.

After a quick shower, I go into my room and throw on a tank top and shorts before going to work on my wet hair. The door to my room flies open, and I gasp. Noel

166

struts in wearing a towel. My jaw hangs a little as I take in the sight of his bare chest and tattooed arms. If it wasn't for my self imposed kissing only rules, I'd be all over him.

He smirks at my expression. "Don't worry. I'm only coming in to get some clothes. We put my bag in here last night before we made a bed on the couch for me, remember?"

I swallow hard, still unable to look away from his body. He notices me staring, and his smile turns wickedly sexy. Noel starts toward me like a tiger stalking prey with slow and deliberate movements. The sight of his approach causes my stomach to knot.

Quickly, I sit on my bed, hoping that will stop him form coming any closer. I don't know how much longer I can keep telling him no and actually mean it.

Noel sits down beside me and twists around, holding his towel in place with one hand, to look into my eyes. "What do you say, Lane. We have the house all to ourselves. We're in your old room. It'll be just like old times."

"Noel…" I warn.

He ignores me and cups my face, leans in and kisses me. There's purpose behind this kiss. It's soft, yet rough enough to mean business.

I close my eyes, and my fingers find their way into the hair on the nape of his neck. Noel pushes me down on the bed and kisses a trail down my neck. The scruff on his chin scratches against my skin. He pulls the strap of my tank top down and kisses my collar bone. A ripple of pure pleasure jets clear down into my toes. I grab his face in my hands and pull his mouth back to mine. This kiss feels desperate, like we need each other more than air. I want to be closer to him. I can't get enough.

"Fuck the kissing only rule, Lane. I need you. Be with me, please."

I close my eyes as I melt from his pleading words.

Noel helps me out of my shirt and then slides his large hands down the length of my torso. He sits back on his heels in the bed and reaches for the button on my shorts. My body writhes against the bed, begging for him to undress me.

He pops the button open and unzips my jean shorts. Noel bends at the waist and kisses the hollow of my throat. A moan escapes me as he works his way down to my breasts. His index finger runs along the lace at the top of the cup of my bra.

"These are so nice," he says as he peels back my bra. My nipples stand erect from the chill and he smiles. "So nice." He wraps his lips around one and sucks.

I arch my back. His mouth on me feels amazing. "Noel…"

"Tell me," he murmurs against my nipple. "Tell me how much you want me—only me."

He slides his hand down my stomach and shoves my shorts down around my thighs. His tongue swirls around my pink nipple and I shiver. "God…Noel!"

"Say it," he commands—his breath hot against my skin.

"I want you, Noel. I need you." I should feel self-conscious about saying that, but I don't care because it's the truth.

"Yes, baby. Only me," he growls against my skin and shoves his hand down inside my panties.

"Only you, Noel," I cry. "Oh, God."

"Damn, you are so wet," he whispers. "I want to bury myself in you so deep."

Noel's fingers slide against my wet flesh, before he dips a finger inside of me. I moan and arch against the palm of his hand. He works his finger in and out a few times before slipping in another. His steady motion makes me pant. If I wasn't in desperate need for him I would be embarrassed by my loud breathing, but at this point, I don't care. I want him so much.

He pulls out and flicks my clit, and I nearly explode on the spot.

I sit up and reach for the towel. It falls from around his waist and onto the bed. He is ready for me, hard and standing at attention. I grab the base of him and stroke. The memory of him inside me long ago, floods me. I lick my lips and stretch forward and take the tip of him in my mouth. Noel sucks in a quick breath through his teeth, and the sound make my insides quiver with need.

I relax and suck him in as far as I can. "That feels so fucking good, baby."

The need to please him fills me to the brim. I take my mouth away and say, "Lay back."

I crawl to his side and slide the hair away from my face, so he can watch me take his hard length into my mouth again. He moans and lets out of string of soft curse words before shoving his head back against a pillow.

Sleeping with him goes against everything I've been telling myself since I agreed to this job, but it feels right, like there's nothing else.

Noel slides a finger under my panties and massages the sensitive flesh between my swollen cleft. A need builds inside me—a need to have him inside me, thrusting deep, trying to reach my core. Heat floods me as he strokes my clit. A tremor shoots though my whole body as I come, moaning around his cock.

Noel sits up and lifts my chin and claims my mouth with his. "Lane, I want to be inside you, but more than anything I want to come inside you. Are you on the pill?"

My breath came out in a heavy pant. "Yes."

I don't ask anything else because I don't care. I want him so much it actually hurts.

He shoves me back against the bed and kisses me like I'm his world. His lips scorch me as they trail their way down my neck. It feels so good. I don't want this feeling to ever go away.

Noel's tongue darts out and licks my nipple before he nips it teasingly between his teeth. I gasp from the sensual pain, and he looks up at me and grins before working his way down further. The muscles in my right leg tenses as he throws it over his shoulder. A finger slides inside of me as he sucks my most sensitive flesh between his lips.

An ache builds inside me again. "Noel, oh God. I'm going to come."

This only encourages him. He laps between my folds and when he flicks his tongue I cry out. Release floods me as my second orgasm rips through me, and I grab a fist full of Noel's hair.

Before I have a chance to fully recover Noel grabs my hips and pulls me toward him. He shoves the head of his cock inside me and groans. "Fuck. Lane. Oh my God, you're so fucking tight. I already want to come."

His fingers dig into my hips as he pushes all the way in me. I bite my lip to keep from crying out. The feel of him inside me, stretching me, lights me on fire. The sound of his skin smacking mine fills the room as he drives into me. I grab my boobs to keep them from bouncing. Noel growls in approval and pumps even faster and harder.

I lift my hips to meet his, and he shuts his eyes. He's close and I can feel my own need building for the third time. "Lane, fuck. I've missed you so much."

I run my fingers through his hair. "I've missed you, too."

His mouth claims mine in a quick kiss before I feel the muscles in his back tense under my fingers. A primal growl emits from his throat, and he bites his lip in ecstasy as he erupts inside me, filling me full.

He collapses on top of me and buries his face in the crook of my neck. A content sigh comes out of his mouth before he leans up and kisses my lips. I feel exactly the same. Noel removes himself from me and rolls onto his side. His large hands pull me close and runs his nose runs across my jaw. "That was…wow."

"Mmmm," I sigh in agreement.

His fingers trail across my stomach, and I slide closer into his body. The slightest little movement from him causes my body to crave more. I can't believe I'm lying in his arms, post-bliss, after the most amazing sex I've ever had.

Noel laughs. "Who knew we didn't have a clue what we were doing back then. It's a wonder you didn't dump me for my lack of sexual skills."

I hate when we talk about our break-up, all the time we missed together. How many other women have lain in this exact spot with Noel since then? Ten, twenty . . . a hundred? I cringe.

"Like I had a lot of bragging room." I smile at him while I try to push thoughts of the past out of my mind.

He props himself up on his elbow and twirls a lock of my hair around his finger. "I've been wondering something, but I don't want you to get angry with me."

I run my fingers along the stubble on his chin. "I won't get angry with you, Noel. I promise. You can ask me anything."

"Have you been with anyone else other than me? I know four years is a long time and I suspect you have been, but I was just curious. It doesn't matter to me if you were."

I wish I'd never been with Cory, the only boyfriend I've had since Noel. He's the worst thing about my past. He almost made me never want to trust men again.

Noel's thumb runs over my cheek. "What are you thinking?" He kisses my shoulder. "Tell me, please. If something is bothering you, I want you to talk to me about it."

I turn my head and stare into his blue eyes. It would kill me if things didn't work out. Cory nearly ruined me. A relationship is built on trust, and he has to know everything about my past. Honesty is the one thing I discovered is a necessity for something to work between two people. "I've only been with one person since you."

He raises his eyebrows in surprise. "One? That's it?"

I smack his arm. "Why would you expect more? You know I'm not that way." I look away from him. "And I regret that one to tell you the truth."

Noel rolls onto his back and stares up at the ceiling. "I knew you were too fucking good for me, Lane."

This time I roll over and stare down at him. "Don't say that. If anything you are too good for me."

He shakes his head. "No, I'm really not. You're perfect and sweet. A good girl. I'm just going to taint you."

"You're not." I try to reassure him and grab his face. I stare into his eyes. "If anyone tainted me, it was my ex. You'll never treat me the way he did. I know you wouldn't. Don't ever think that you're too good for me. Ever."

He frowns. "What did he do to you?"

I glance away. The pain from my memory still cuts deep. It is the ultimate betrayal. "I walked in on him having sex with another girl in his dorm room."

Noel's eyes soften and he sits up. His arms wrap around me. "I'm so sorry, Lane. Were you with him long?"

I nod while Noel strokes the bare skin on my back. "A little over two years. He was my first real college friend, and it turned into more. I thought I knew him. I never dreamed he was screwing every girl he could get his hands on behind my back."

"Want me to kick his ass?"

I laugh. "I'd prefer to never talk about him again. It's in the past."

Noel smiles. "That's fine with me. I'll never do you wrong, Lane. You know that, right? No matter what you hear about me, just know there isn't another girl that could ever compare to you. You're all that I want. Don't believe anything other than that."

I think about all the pictures I've seen on the internet—Noel with a different woman in each one. "Are you telling me you don't get around? I saw you with the two blonde bimbos myself, remember?"

He frowns. "I'm not saying there weren't other women. There were some, but like in my sick, twisted mind they were all you. I've never stopped loving you, Lane. I didn't think I ever had another shot with you. You left me, remember? I tried to get over you, but I couldn't."

My heart flops in my chest. It doesn't matter how many women he's slept with since we were apart. All that matters now is that he's mine, and he only wants me. I can see it in his eyes. He means what he's telling me.

Noel pushes my hair back and cups my face. "I love you, Lane. I always have."

That's all I need to hear. I melt into his touch. "I love you, too."

His lips crush mine and he pushes me down on the bed. Noel settles his body on top of mine and I can feel his erection slide up against me. I smile against his lips before we make love one more time.

Chapter 15

After finishing up the final touches for dinner, I help bring the food out with Mom. I set the bowl holding the potato salad on the table, out on the back deck and she brings out the salad. I glance over at Noel, who stands watch over the grill, and smile. He's grinning while he stares at the steaks, and I wonder if he's thinking about the incredible sex we just had in my room.

The kissing rule didn't last very long, but I'm not one bit upset over it.

"Honey." Mom touches my arm. "I didn't think you two were back together."

I shrug and bit my lip. "Things change."

Mom nods and her eyes light up at the conformation. "I thought so. That boy is still crazy over you."

A fierce blush creeps up my neck and floods my cheeks. "Yeah, well, I know exactly how he feels."

The doorbell rings before she can dig for any additional details and I'm grateful. It's hard to explain a relationship status I'm even unsure about.

Muffled conversation comes from inside the house, and Noel turns away from the grill. He grins when his mother steps outside. Instantly he's in front of her, wrapping her up in a big bear-hug. Warmth spreads all over me, and I choke back a tear. I'm glad I made this happen.

"Noel, honey, it's so good to see you." His mom, Irene, pats him on the back while still in his embrace.

His smile causes his eyes to twinkle. "You too, Mom. I've missed you so much. I can't believe it's been so long."

Irene pulls back and touches her son's cheek. "Let's not wait another four years, okay." She glances in my direction with tears streaming down her face. "Lanie, get over here and give me a hug."

She wraps her slender arms around me and whispers in my ear, "Thank you for bringing me back my boy."

When she decides to let go, she flips her dark hair over her shoulder and I can't help but to smile at how many features Noel takes from his mom. The hair color, the ocean-clear blue eyes, and a heart warming smile.

Noel grabs the steaks off the grill while the rest of us find a seat. He sits between me and Irene and fills us in about life on the road.

"I've been curious, Noel. How did you meet your other band-mates? I've seen pictures of all you boys, and I don't remember any of them from around here," my mom says.

Noel swallows down the steak he is chewing and glances quickly at Irene. "On the road. After high school, I traveled for a while."

I frown knowing that isn't exactly what happened, but I know he's trying to keep Irene from having to explain why her husband exiled his own son. Noel knows no matter what I did, Mom would never cut me out of her life like that. The problems between him and his father were always something I kept from her, so she wouldn't understand the underlying tension in their relationship.

Mom lifts her brow. "Really? Irene, I don't know how you and Frank kept sane. Jim and I would've been out of our minds worried about Lanie if she took off like that being so young."

Irene's lips twist, like she's fighting back a sob. "It wasn't really up to me."

Noel grabs her hand in his. "It's okay, Mom. I know it wasn't your fault."

She can't stop herself this time. Irene buries her face into a napkin and lets out a soft sob. "Yes, it is. I should've stopped your father from kicking you out. It wasn't right. Just because you refused to go to college like he wanted, didn't give him the right to take you away from me," Irene sighs. "He misses you, you know. I told him you were here, and he wants to see you."

He pulls his lips into a tight line, but doesn't answer.

Irene waits on Noel's response, but I can tell by the look on his face he doesn't like the turn of this conversation.

"Jesus. Mom…we've been through this. I don't want—"

She pulls her cell phone from her purse. "Let me call him, tell him you're going to come over and talk."

Noel's jaw muscle works under his skin. "No! I went through hell when he threw me out. He knew what I was going through when Lane dumped me, and he told me to leave anyway. He didn't care if I had a place to stay or food to eat. Why the hell should I care about his feelings now?"

"Noel Anthony Falcon," his mom scolds him. "You should give your father a chance. He's sorry."

He rolls his eyes and then stands up abruptly.

"Noel?" his mother questions his action with a little panic in her voice.

He leans down and kisses her on the top of her head. "It was good to see you, Mother."

He leaves without another word or without looking back. I hear the Escalade start in the driveway and then tear down the road.

Mom hugs Irene as she sobs. "He just needs some time. Give him that. He'll come around."

My heart aches both for the pain that I know Noel is going through and for his parents. It's apparent there is still a lot of love there, but both father and son are too damn prideful to be the first to start their reconnection.

An hour rolls past, and Noel still hasn't returned. Mom is out of comforting things to tell Irene at this point and she's still a crying mess. I send a quick text checking on him and it's almost immediately answered.

Back at the bus. Sorry I didn't come back. Just couldn't deal.

I sigh and stuff my phone back in my pocket. "He's back in Dallas."

Irene peers at me through blood shot eyes. "You have to go to him, Lane, and convince him to forgive his father."

"Mrs. Falcon, I don't think it's my—"

"You have to. It's tearing us apart. I can't lose my only son."

She looks miserable, and I hurt for her.

I notice Mom's face. Her head tilted slightly to the right and her face scrunches. It's the same look I've seen countless times since Dad passed away. It's hard to lose a loved one. I've learned just how difficult it can be, and I don't want something to happen to his father while this huge rift is between them. I know it would kill him.

For Noel's own sake, I need to try and at least get him to talk to his dad.

I rub my forehead. I have no clue how I'm going to get him to agree to this. "Okay. I'll do my best. No promises."

His mother reaches across the table and grabs my hand. "Thank you."

****

The bus is oddly quiet when I return to Dallas. I open the bedroom door and find Noel lying on the bed. His arm drapes over his beautiful face while taking in deep, sleeping breaths. I set my bag on the floor and then crawl in bed beside him. I wrap my arms around his stomach and rest my chin on his chest.

He removes his arm from his face and smiles sheepishly. "Hi. You're not pissed at me?"

I shake my head. "Why would I be mad at you? I understand why you left."

He traces the bare skin on my arm with his fingers. "You do?"

"Your mom shouldn't force you to talk to Frank. I know you'll do it when you're ready."

He closes his eyes. "That's just it. I don't think I'll ever be able to do that."

"Why? I'm sure you two can find a way to forgive each other."

Noel's eyes narrow. "Forgive me? I didn't do a damn thing to that man."

The anger, clear to see on his face, startles me. I sit up and sit Indian style. "I didn't say you did. I just know sometimes saying sorry, even if it's not your fault, goes a long way in smoothing out a fight."

He leans up on both elbows. "I will never tell that man sorry. You don't know the cruel things he said to me the night he kicked me out."

Noel throws both of his legs over the bed and sits with his back to me. Just when I think he's going to let me into that brain of his, he shuts me out.

I frown. "What did he say?"

Both shoulders slump, and he takes a deep breath. "He said..."—he clears his throat—"he said I was one huge mistake. That all I've ever been is a disappointment to him."

His shoulders shake, and I know he's crying.

I slide beside him and wrap my arms around him. "I'm sorry," I whisper.

He wipes his eyes with the palm of his hands and sniffs. "I don't know why I'm being such a fucking baby about this."

I kiss his cheek. "Don't be ashamed to share your feelings with me."

He turns his head and rests his forehead against mine. The scent of him surrounds me and I can't help to think about earlier in the day, when we had amazing sex in my bedroom. I inhale deeply and close my eyes. Noel leans in, and brushes his mouth against mine and then works his way down my jaw line. I can tell he's thinking about this afternoon as well.

I stifle a moan as his tongue traces the sensitive skin over my pulse point. I run my fingers into his hair as I feel the arousal between my legs build.

"Lane…I need you." Suddenly his mouth is on mine, and his hands tug at the button on my shorts. He slips his tongue in my mouth, and a low groan emits from the back of his throat. The taste of him shoots a thrill through me, and I push his shirt up before shoving him back on the bed. I kiss every inch of his abs before he sits up and helps me out of my shirt. He unclasps my bra and tugs it down so my breasts spring free.

Noel wraps his lips around my protruding nipple and the moan I held back earlier, escapes me. Every inch of me burns with an intense fire for him. Eager hands tear at my shorts after he pulls his shirt over his broad shoulders.

We roll over and he pins my arms above my head. His lips attack mine in a hot frenzy. He pulls back, stands up and seizes my hips toward him, sliding me across the bed. I lift my hips as he grips the waistband of my shorts and panties and removes them from my body. I sit up and slip my hands inside his jeans and shove them down, revealing his perfect ass.

A lazy grin spreads across his face as he steps out of his pants and climbs on top of me.

"I want you to be mine," he says in a husky voice as he glides his fingers against my slick folds.

An ache fills me. I need this man. I need him in my heart and inside my body. No matter the tension or the job. I want to be his.

"I'm yours," I say against his lips.

I cry out as he dips a finger inside me. Pleasure rolls through every nerve and inner muscles ripple then clench around him. Every stroke of his finger fans the fire within. When his thumb encircles my clit, I toss my head back in ecstasy as I explode around him.

"God, you're so fucking hot when you come." His tongue flicks against my nipple.

He kisses my lips and sinks his hips between my thighs. His pressing cock teases my moist heat and causes me to squirm. Both of my arms encircle his body, and my hands run down the rigid muscles in his back.

One swift thrust and he's inside me. A shudder rips through me as he growls. The steady grinding of his hips causes the ache to build in my core again. Each penetration seems slow and deliberate, like he's savoring making me his.

His blue eyes stare into mine and I run my fingers along his jaw. He leans into my palm and closes his eyes as he pumps his hips faster. The mattress moves with every thrust and I lift my bottom up off to meet his hips, allowing him to fill me further.

A second orgasm rips through me. "Oh, God."

This only excites him, and he increases the rhythm. Sweat beads across his face and he bites his lip. "You feel so fucking good."

He's holding back, I can see it in his face. "Let go for me."

He shakes his head. "I want to make this last. I don't want it to end."

I bring his mouth down to mine and kiss him deeply. "I'm not going anywhere. Let go."

As soon as the last word leaves my mouth, he cries out in pure pleasure. "Lane. Oh fuck."

Warmth feels me as I let go one last time with him. Noel erupts inside me, filling me with his hot seed after one final thrust. His entire body shivers, and he collapses on top of me. Soft kisses cover both of my cheeks and then finally my lips.

Chapter 16

Noel's steady breathing tells me he's asleep. I roll over on my side and watch the beautiful man beside me. Who knew my heart is capable of holding so much love for one person?

My stomach rumbles and I remember I never ate dinner earlier thanks to Noel and his antics. Being on this bus with him for the rest of this two week period is going to be crazy.

I push myself up from bed and Noel reaches for me. "Where are you going?"

I rub his arm. "I'm just going to try to find something to eat. I'm starving."

He frowns with his eyes closed. "We probably don't have much out there. I'm sorry, Lane. I can send someone to pick you up something."

He's unbelievably sweet. "No, that's okay. I'm sure I can find something." I bend down and kiss his cheek. "Go back to sleep, baby."

He smiles and pulls me into him and kisses my lips. "Hurry back."

Reluctantly, I pull away from Noel's warm embrace, and he rolls onto his side. The clothes I had on earlier are flung around the room. I find my underwear on the floor and slip them on along with one of Noel's cotton t-shirts. The cloth runs over my nose, and I breathe it in. It still smells like him.

I turn back to watch him. He's already fallen back to sleep.

I open the door and peak out. The lights are dim and all the curtains on the foxholes are drawn tight. The sound of the guys all returning to the bus earlier had woken me up, so I figure they are lingering around somewhere.

A couple of the snores come from the bunks as I walk past and I chuckle. The twins are obviously out for the count after their two day spread of groupie sex.

Once inside the kitchen, I'm surprised to see Aubrey and Riff snuggling together on the loveseat. I thought she was at her parents by now.

They examine me as I come into their view.

I do my best to ignore them and head straight for the little kitchen area, and hope they'll do the same for me.

No such luck.

Riff stands and pulls Aubrey up with him. I roll my eyes as they plop down at the bench seat at the table. I squat down and look through the cabinets. The fabric from Noel's shirt is big enough that it hangs down to my thighs, but I wish I would have put some shorts on. The fact that I can feel Riff's eyes boring into my back has me on edge.

A cabinet door shuts behind me and I glance in their direction. Riff sits down with a package full of Oreos at the table. The rumble in my stomach is audible. What I wouldn't give for one of those cookies right now. He peels back the wrapper and my mouth waters.

"Make yourself useful and grab us some milk from the fridge," Riff says. "I always keep it in there. The guys know better than to take my stuff."

Sure enough, there's a gallon of two percent white milk in there. I sit it on the counter and search for a couple glasses.

"There should be some plastic cups on the stop shelf, above the sink," Riff informs me as I poke around.

There's only one cup left in the bag, and my heart sinks. Damn. Oreos aren't the same without milk. I pour the milk into it for Riff and walk over to the table. I set the cup down, and slide into the seat across from them.

He pushes the package across the table to me. "You don't want some milk, too?"

I shrug and pull out a cookie. "Only one cup."

Riff smiles and puts his cup in the middle. "We can share it—just no double dipping. I heard where your mouth's been."

Aubrey smacks his arm. "Sorry, Lanie, but you were kind of loud."

Heat rises up my neck, and my face flushes. It never occurred to me that I'm loud enough for the guys on the bus to hear Noel and I having sex, but it is obvious they could. I mean, I heard every single moan when they had their parties in full swing on the other side of the door. How could I be so naive to think they couldn't hear me too?

Riff chuckles and dunks a cookie in the milk. "Nothing to be embarrassed about, it was fucking hot. Noel's one lucky son of a bitch."

Aubrey giggles and then winks at me.

I cover my face with my hand. "Oh, God."

Riff bites into his cookie. "You say that a lot, don't you?"

My head snaps up. "Can we please stop talking about this? It's not exactly the kind of conversation I should be having with you guys."

He shrugs. "You know, about the ticket thing, I'm sorry. You did try to blow me off. I didn't think you meant it. I thought it was your angle."

"My angle?"

Riff nods. "Most chicks play games with me. You weren't the first girl who tried to play the hard-to-get card with me. I figured you read one of my interviews where I said that turned me on."

The tension I feel towards him melts a little with his apology. He seems sincere, and since he put it that way, I could see why he thought I'm a groupie.

I dip my cookie in the milk, too. "An interviewer actually asked what your turn-ons were?"

"You wouldn't believe some of the shit we get asked. Noel gets the worst of it, though, being the front man and all. People are constantly trying to dig things up on him, but he's good at keeping his life secret."

I swallow the food down. "It's not like Noel has a lot of dirt to find."

Riff raises his eyebrows. "How long has it been since you dated him?"

"A little over four years. Why?"

Riff looks away from me and takes out another cookie. "A lot can happen in four years, Lanie."

What is that suppose to mean? Is he saying there is a lot of dirt on Noel—dirt that even my hours of internet stalking didn't uncover? Noel is a good guy. I don't buy it.

I shrug. "I'm sure Noel isn't intentionally hiding things from me. We all have our pasts and secrets we don't want people to know."

Riff's eyes scan my face. "We most certainly do."

Riff pops the last Oreo in his mouth. His gaze never leaves me, like he's waiting for more questions, but I never ask. Anything in Noel's past is just that, in the past. If there is something I need to know, I'm sure he'll tell me.

Riff stands beside the table and then sticks out his hand. "Truce?"

I smile as his large fingers wrap around my hand. "Truce. I would like that. We should be friends since you and Aubrey...you know."

Riff glances over at my friend and wiggles his eyebrows. "Oh yeah, I know. Friends it is."

When Riff leaves the room, Aubrey turns in my direction. She smirks and I shake my head. "Don't you shake your head at me, missy. I told you all about mine, now it's your turn to dish. It sounded like it was incredible!"

I pinch the bridge of my nose. "Aubrey..."

She yanks my hands away from my face. "Stop it. Don't be embarrassed. You had a good time—nothing wrong with that, Lanie. So, tell me, does he get his Sex-god title back now?"

I roll my eyes and smile.

She smacks the table and grins. "I knew it. That guy is sex on a stick."

Aubrey stays on the bus with Riff and me until it's ready to head to the next stop on the tour. Riff walks her out to the car, no doubt for a hot goodbye make-out session. I'll miss her, but I only have a week or so left until I'll see her all the time.

That thought makes me a little sad. It also means I only have a week left with Noel.

****

The next morning I awake in Noel's bed. His arm holds me tight against his side. Warm breath wafts rhythmically against my neck. The smell of his skin so close intoxicates me, and I find myself craving to be closer to him. I trace my fingertips along the tattoos on his forearm—each one fading into the next. Both of his arms are living pieces of artwork. Beautiful.

Noel nudges my neck with his nose. "Mmmmm. I want to wake up like this every morning."

I smile, and my insides turn into mush. "Me too. I love being here with you."

He kisses my neck and rubs the bare skin on my arm. "Good because I plan on keeping you here forever."

I roll to face him. "Forever?"

His blue eyes peer up at me through impossibly long and sexy eyelashes. "Afraid so. I'm addicted to you. There's no way I can be without this now."

I giggle and kiss his lips. He is simply the most amazing man on the plant. How did I ever get so lucky? "What do you think will keep me here?"

The softness of his lips against my jaw makes my toes curl. I wiggle closer against him. Noel's hot skin against mine is maddening. I hitch my leg over his hip, and he runs his hand up my calf then hooks around my knee. His hard length presses against me through my underwear and I gasp.

Noel smiles and grinds himself into me. "This."

A moan escapes from my lips, and Noel's mouth claims mine. I claw at his back as he rolls on top of me. His hand shoves up the t-shirt that I put on last night—my naked breasts on display for him. Noel's eyes roam over my chest before he dips down and sucks one of my nipples into his mouth. Oh, God his tongue can do wondrous things.

Noel chuckles against my skin. "Quiet, baby. The guys are still asleep out there."

I slap my hand over my mouth. Am I being loud again? How embarrassing.

Noel kisses a trail down my stomach, and I sigh. His fingers grip my underwear on each side of my hips and he pulls them off of me. I laugh when he tosses them over his shoulder and smirks. The expressions on his face sometimes are down right sexy.

I grin and close my eyes, full of anticipation of what comes next.

****

The suite is amazing. I've never been in a hotel this nice. Ever. The bell boy leaves our luggage in the bedroom, and Noel gives the kid a tip. His eyes light up, and he thanks Noel profusely before leaving our room. My Noel, always a nice guy.

Noel wraps his arms around my waist and I thread my fingers into his hair. "That's nice of you."

He smiles and shrugs. "I know what it's like working for every dollar you get. If a hundred dollar bill makes the kid's day, it's the least I can do."

I kiss his lips. "You are unbelievably sweet, you know that?"

"Speaking of sweet." Noel sighs. "The Kid's Wish Foundation contacted me yesterday and asked me to visit a little boy with Leukemia. They told me I'm his idol and his wish is to meet me."

"That's amazing, Noel. When do you get to meet him?"

"Tomorrow. The organization booked a flight for me right after tonight's show to Tucson."

My heart sinks a little at the thought of not being with him for a day.

He tilts my chin up and gazes down at me. "It's only for one night. I'll be back before you know it. Besides, your boss is flying in tomorrow. You have to stick around and find out what exactly you marketing types need to do with Black Falcon's charity to get it off the ground."

"You owe me close to a thousand hours for all these kisses, you know."

He laughs. "Hours well spent if you ask me. You have full control of the charity, Lane. I know you'll do what you think is best and it will be amazing."

I lay my head into his chest. His kindness knows no limits. "You are the most amazing person I know."

He chuckles and kisses the top of my head. "Right back at ya."

We stay locked in each others arms for a few moments. The steady thud of his heart beats keep time in my ear. My fingers move down and trace the taut muscles in his shoulders. I don't think a more perfect man exists. Noel can have any woman in the world, and yet he chooses me. I wonder if that officially makes me the luckiest girl on the planet.

He twirls a lock of my hair around his finger. "What do you want to do today?"

I pull back and lick my lips. Noel smiles as I run an index finger down his chest. "Oh, I don't know. What did you have in mind?"

His gaze smolders as he runs his tongue over his top lip. "I have lots of things in mind that I would like to do to you, but I'm afraid you just might break me if we keep up this pace. You're insatiable."

A shudder ripples through me. Oh how I would like to have him try all those things on me, but he's right. If we keep this up we'll never see the light of day again. We've had sex three amazing times. Noel is the insatiable one, or well, just as bad as me. My last boyfriend never had the stamina for more than once a day.

I grin and look up at him. "You're right. We should get something to eat. I can't live on Oreos alone."

Noel's eyes widen. "Shit. Now I have to buy Riff more. He gets all bitchy if someone eats his food."

"I don't think he minded. He gave them to me."

Noel's brow furrowed. "He was up with you last night?"

His body tenses under my touch. The tension whenever Riff's name comes up is so odd. The anger between them clearly hasn't left his system. "Yeah, he and Aubrey both, and he actually apologized again for the golden ticket thing."

Noel shoves his lips into a thin line and runs his hand through his hair. "Did he say anything else?"

The thought crosses my mind to ask him about the dirt that Riff implied he has, but the look on Noel's face stops me. He looks angry, and I don't understand his problem with Riff. He always tells me his band mates are his brothers. The way he's acting at the mention of Riff talking to me, isn't very brotherly love-like.

I place my hands on Noel's shoulders. "Are you okay? Is there something we need to talk about?"

Noel flinches like I just smacked him in the face. "No. Why? Do you think we have something we need to discuss?"

His tone catches me off guard. Why is he so defensive all of the sudden? Is he really keeping things from me like Riff implied?

I drop my hands from his chest. "No. I guess not."

I turn to walk away from him, but he catches my hand. "Hey…are you mad at me?"

I shake my head. "Of course not. I just don't understand why you are getting so angry."

He sighs and pulls me back against his body. "I'm sorry. I'm not mad at you. Riff can push my buttons like no other. I don't want him around you when I'm not there."

Maybe he isn't hiding anything after all.

I trace his jaw with my fingers. "You may not trust Riff, but you need to trust me. There's no one I want other than you. Nothing he can say will ever change that."

Noel pulls my hand away from his face and kisses my fingertips. "I don't want to lose you, Lane. The thought of it scares the shit out of me."

"Me too. I can't believe we're together again. Nothing is going to break us up this time." My voice sounds firm.

His large hands cup my face and his thumbs rub against my cheeks. His blue eyes search my face. "Promise?" Noel whispers.

I don't look away from his gaze. "I promise."

Noel's mouth crushes against mine as the words leave my lips. The heat bounds between us and my hands fly up into his thick, dark hair. His hands slide up, under my t-shirt and stroke the flesh on the small of my back.

I moan and Noel chuckles. "I love that you get turned on so fast for me. It's unbelievably sexy. How come you weren't like this in high school?"

I kiss his lips and shrug. "Scared, I guess, and inexperienced."

He grins. "What do you expect from two virgins?"

He cuddles me tighter and I smile. "True, but I'm glad it was you."

"Me too."

We spend the rest of the day hanging out in our room. Most of our time in each others arms making future plans and filling in the blanks between us from the last few years.

The food from our room service order is devoured quickly.

"Are you excited that your boss will be here tomorrow?" Noel asks.

I swallow down the last bite of my hamburger from room service before answering. "Excited and nervous."

He tilts his head to the side. "Why nervous? You already have the job locked down."

"I know, but I really want Diana to like me. If she finds out that we are…together, she may not take me so seriously."

People from all over the globe request Diana for projects. She has the magic touch. It seems like everything she gets her hands on turns into a world wide phenomenon.

I can only dream of having a career like hers one day.

He touches my cheek. "How could she not love you? You are the best person I know. You're straight laced—head always in the right direction. I pretty much think you're perfect. And who doesn't love perfection?"

My face blushes and I look away. He thinks I'm perfect. The most perfect man in the world thinks I'm perfect. Someone is going to pinch me soon because this is too much like a damn dream.

"I'm nowhere near perfect, Noel."

Noel nods and touches my nose with his fingertip. "You are to me." He hops off the bed. "I have to take a shower and get ready to meet up with the guys for sound check."

I gaze up to him and grin. "I suppose you want me to wash your back?"

He wiggles his eyebrows suggestively. "That would be nice…among other things."

I laugh and chuck a pillow at him as he heads towards the bathroom. The faded jeans he's wearing hugs his back side just right and I appreciate the view. How did I ever get so lucky?

My cell phone rings the minute Noel shut the bathroom door. I fish it out of my purse by the third ring. The caller's name appears on the screen and I smile as I answer.

"Too busy to call me this morning or what? I need some juicy details. I'm dying over here," Aubrey says.

I giggle. "Well, I was a little…preoccupied."

"Score one for the Sex-God. I bet he's amazing."

I'm silent for few seconds and I know the suspense is killing Aubrey. "You know how they say things get better with time…"

Aubrey shrieks into the phone. "Gah! You are so lucky. He's amazingly hot, sweet, and now we can add great in bed to the list. You know I'm jealous, right?"

"Why are you jealous? You and Riff have a thing."

She sighs. "A thing is right. The thing that boy can do with his tongue…"

"Okay. Okay. I don't want to hear about your Sexual Olympics."

She laughs into the phone, just as Noel pokes his head out of the bathroom door. I frown and point to the phone so he knows I won't be coming in. He rolls his eyes and closes the door.

I catch up with Aubrey for the next few minutes about her family. She keeps turning the conversation back to Riff. She's asked me at least twenty times in the last few minutes if he's asked about her or not.

After I convince her that Riff is secretly, madly in love with her she finally let's me off the phone.

Noel steps into the large bedroom area wearing nothing but a towel. Water droplets speckle his chest and the smell of his body wash fills the room. He lays a clean pair of jeans and a t-shirt on the bed next to me and my eyes trail over his body like it's dessert. It really is spectacular the way his muscles bulge under his skin. It's practically art—the naughty kind that women love to drool over.

Noel laughs and I jerk my head back down to the laptop. I know he's caught me staring, but it's hard not to.

He pulls on his jeans, with no underwear, and throws on his shirt. Men are so lucky. They can look yummy in less than fifteen minutes.

After I'm ready, we head out of our love nest holding hands. Noel's thumb strokes the skin on the back of my hand. This small gesture is somehow the most reassuring thing in the world.

A black town car with tinted windows waits at the entrance of the hotel. The driver, wearing a black suit, nods at Noel before opening the back door for us. Noel helps me into the car then slides in next to me. The driver shuts us in and hops in the front.

The smooth car pulls out onto the road. It's crazy Noel has so much money he doesn't even have to drive himself around like a normal person anymore.

"Do you still have your car?" I ask Noel.

His eyes sparkle a little at the mention of his black Chevelle. "Yep. She's tucked away in my garage."

His garage? "I didn't know you owned a place."

He wraps his arm around me and trails his fingers over the bare skin on my shoulder. "Yeah, I bought a house in Kentucky a couple years ago with the first big chunk of money I got from the record company."

I tilt my head to the side and gaze up at him. "Why Kentucky?"

He shrugs. "Why not? No one really bothers me there. Who would expect that I'd live there? Plus, the rest of the guys in the band are from the area, so I got a place near them. I like the space. It's peaceful there, you know. Reminds me a lot of where we grew up."

"It has a lake?"

He grins. "Yep, and the dock there puts our little one to shame."

"I'd love to see it sometime."

His eyes lock on mine. "One day soon. Maybe after you see it, you'll want to stay."

My breath catches and I'm stunned. Did Noel just ask me to move in with him? It's true we've known each other our entire life, but we just got back together. Am I ready for such a huge leap?

Noel runs his hand through his hair. "Every time I feel like we are moving forward, you throw me off when you freeze up like this. Like you're not quite sure enough about me yet to take things to the next level."

I'm taken back. How could he possibly know I even have the slightest hint of reservation? "Noel...I..."

He leaves one arm around my shoulder and threads my fingers with his free hand. "It's okay, Lane. I know I am moving kind of fast, but I can't seem to help myself. All I want to do is be with you. Now that I have you back, I can't see my life without you. When I think about my future, I think about you."

I want to be with Noel, but I don't want to ruin this by rushing things. We've only been reconnected for a couple days, there's so much I don't know about him anymore. Four years in the rock world pretty much equals ten in the real one. Everything is always on the move here.

The most I can offer him is honesty at this point. "I want to be with you, too. I really do. But I think we need to take things slow. I mean, there's no rush, right?"

Noel's shoulders sag. "I guess not."

He looks away from me and I know I've hurt him. The familiar pain of heart break tears in my chest. I touch his cheek. "I'm not saying I'll never move in, or that it'll even take that long. I'm just saying let's see how the next couple of months go and then we can start talking about moving in together. For now, I'm here. And for now, I'm yours."

He turns those powerful blue eyes on me and nods. "If that's all you can give me for now, then I'll take it."

I know it probably won't take me until the end of the week to feel the same way Noel does, but for now, we need to take it slow. I'm just glad he understands my side of things. Noel never was a very patient person. He's always been an all or nothing type of guy, this compromising side of him is new, but I like it. It shows he's grown.

I kiss his lips, just as we reach the arena Black Falcon will play at tonight. It's another mammoth building, but nowhere near as big as the huge soccer stadium they just filled back in Ohio. It's only my sixth day on the road with him, but I can see how a different city every night would get a little tiresome.

The car comes to a stop beside Big Bertha. Trip sits on a short concert retaining wall across from the bus and slaps his thighs with drum sticks—Tyke beside him with a hood over his head fiddling with his phone.

Noel helps me out of the car and grabs my hand. I smile and glance over at him. His eyes watch me intently as he runs his thumb over the back of my hand. There's something on his mind. I can tell. Years of being friends with a man do have some benefits.

My smile fades. "Are you alright?"

He runs a hand through his hair and then scrubs it over his face. "Yeah, just tired, I guess."

I don't buy his story, but I don't want to rehash the same issue from the car ride over here, if that's what's still on his mind. Hopefully, he really does understand and respect my need to take things slow. I've found most of the things I've done in a rush never work out. Prime example: breaking up with him the first time.

We just need time.

Trip notices us and nods his head. "What's up love birds?"

Noel smirks at the black haired drummer. "Did you guys hang out here all day?"

"Yeah, pretty much. This little town is boring as hell. They don't even have a fucking Starbucks close. Can you believe that shit?" Trip rolls his eyes at the city's lameness. "The only thing to do is hang out on Bertha and play Xbox. Did you go over to the hotel?"

"Lane and I did."

Trip grins. "Damn, dude. You're a machine."

The skin on my face burns. I know it's beet red. Did everyone on the bus hear everything we did yesterday?

Trip laughs and Noel shoves him back. The force of the playful shove sends Trip back against the shrubs behind him. That only causes him to laugh harder and his brother, Tyke to join in.

Noel pulls me by the hand toward the bus. "Ignore them. The more they see it gets to you, the more they'll keep at it."

I want to die.

I've never been one who is overly sexual or boisterous about my sex life, so to suddenly have everyone on the planet…okay, maybe not the planet, but definitely the band and most of the Black Flacon crew know Noel and I have been at it like rabbits since yesterday, bothers me. It's totally embarrassing.

Noel opens the bus door and leads me inside. It's surprisingly clean today and it smells like a cleaner of some sort and air freshener. This is most certainly a different, yet welcomed, sight to what we left this morning.

Noel notices the look on my face and grins. "Told you we'd get this cleaned up. We aren't total animals, you know."

The toilet flushes and my eyes scan the hallway, curious as to who is back there. Riff steps out, wearing yellow rubber gloves and holding a spray bottle. My eyebrows lift. Riff is the last person on earth I expected as the domestic type.

"You did all this?" I ask Riff.

He shrugs. "I didn't want you to have to live in our filth. Plus…" He pauses and glances to Noel, then back to me. "It's kind of a peace offering for teasing you in front of Aubrey. No hard feelings. Alright?"

I smile. "That's very sweet of you, Riff. Consider it forgotten."

He grins and nods, while Noel stiffens next to me. Clearly, the little act of kindness didn't win him over as easily.

I don't get why Noel is like this with Riff. I figured he'd chill out a little bit after if I reassured him Riff isn't my type. I mean, Riff is kind of with Aubrey now. That alone should relieve his fear.

A ringing cell phone cuts through the tense air. Noel reaches into his pocket and twists his lips. "I have to take this."

He answers the phone and tells the person on the other end to hold on a minute while he makes his way outside.

Riff pulls off the gloves and opens the cabinet beneath the sink. He tosses them in a blue tub along with the cleaner. "I'm going to find Trip. I'll catch you later, Lanie."

Riff pats my shoulder as he slides past me toward the door. I follow him out the door and spot Noel arguing with whoever it is on the phone. It looks heated and it reminds me of the last time I caught him in a heated conversation over business.

Riff stops in front of Noel, and they exchange a few words that I can't make out. Riff shakes his head and walks away. Noel's eyes don't leave him until he's out of sight.

I have the feeling there's way more to their tense relationship than either of them are telling me. This is something I'm going to have to get to the bottom of sooner, rather than later if I'm going to make it on this bus for another week.

Chapter 17

Noel really is amazing on stage. The way he belts out the lyrics sets me in a trance along with the other twenty thousand people here in attendance tonight. I sway to the beat and my head bobs in time to the music. It's so easy to get lost in him.

I don't notice the scantly clad woman in fish net stockings and five inch stiletto heels approach the stage until she's directly beside me. Like me, the woman's eyes fixate on the guys performing. The blonde is pretty much in a black bathing suit covered by a black—what I assume is suppose to be—dress. Only it doesn't cover anything. It's basically strings held together on each side of her body by a three inch piece of black fabric. She's brave. I'll give her that.

I give her a polite smile when she catches me staring at her revealing outfit, and then return my attention back to the stage. I don't know if I'll be able to ever get used to all the women that hang around at shows.

When the song ends, Noel thanks his screaming fans before he glances in my direction.

His smile immediately fades and my eye brows scrunch together. It's the same evil look I catch him giving Riff sometimes.

What's his deal?

The woman beside me has this odd look on her face, too, but she doesn't appear to be mad, in fact, quite the opposite. Some might call it, a shit eating grin, which in my book always equals to up to no good.

The hairs on my arms stand as I wonder how Noel might know this trashy looking chick. Things start to click. He's been with this woman before. Why else would he act like that? Like he's scared that she's next to me. Like she might say something.

My eyes scan the woman a little more closely this time. Her body is amazing, which is probably why she feels the need to show it off in such a manner, but what else could he possibly see in her? For that matter, if he's been with women who look like that, what is he doing with an average girl like me?

She turns toward me and smirks as she notices my stare. I'm tempted to smack it right off her face. "You can run off now." She points her gaze back in Noel's direction. He's still staring at us when she says, "I think we both know who's getting Noel tonight."

The blood boils under my skin and my hands ball into fists. "What?"

She folds her arms over her chest. "Come on. Don't play dumb. We both know I can do way more for him than, well…" She looks me up and down and laughs. "well than you. I'm more his speed. You aren't ready for the big leagues, Princess."

All of my coherent thoughts leave me. I want her to stop talking. Doesn't she think I already know I'm not worthy of Noel. What gives her the right to rub it in my face like this? I don't know where she gets off.

Noel wants me, not her. I know this. I do. But the need to help her shut her mouth rips through me.

I stand there, fists still clenched, praying she just walks away from me.

"Go on." She uncrosses her arms and shoves my shoulder a little.

The second she lays her skanky hand on me I snap. My fist whips up and makes contact with her face before I even realize what I've done. She stumbles back, but manages to stay on her feet. Blood trickles from her right nostril and she wipes it away with her hand.

Her eyes blaze with fury. "You bitch."

The woman lunges for me and shoves my shoulders back. The electrical chords behind me tangle my footing and I fall back. When I hit the floor, she jumps on top of me. A handful of my hair ends up in her hand and she yanks my head to the side before she smacks my face. The blow rattles my skull. I've never been hit before and it surprises me how much it stings. I'm desperate to get her off me. I buck my hips as she draws back to hit me again. Before she has the chance, she flies off me, and I scramble to sit up.

After I'm up on my knees I push forward after her before she has the chance to come back at me first. Two large hands grab under my arms and yank me to my feet.

The adrenaline flows through my veins and my eyes stay locked on the center of my anger. One of the crew members help the blonde up, and I notice the torn 'dress' hangs off her body. The bikini top she has on also moved out of place, exposing one of her nipples.

She readjusts her clothes and scowls at me.

I didn't even notice that the band had stopped playing until that very moment, and every eye in the place, along with every camera, points in my direction.

"Lane! Answer me. Are you okay?" Noel asks. My eyes dart to his face—his brow knitted in confusion and concern. I don't even realize he's holding onto me. "Are you hurt?"

I shake my head and gaze back out toward the crowd. Somehow my little run in with this chick ended up on stage in front of all these people. We must've rolled right on out here.

Trampy girl flips me off before she turns away and a security guard escorts her off the stage.

The mumble of the impatient crowd grows louder as Riff picks up his guitar. "Noel, man, we need to wrap this show up. She's fine."

Noel's mouth pulls into a tight line. He doesn't want to leave me alone right now, but he knows the crowd will rip this place apart if they don't get the show they paid for.

He touches my cheek and I flinch. "Go to the bus and put some ice on that. We'll talk as soon as the set is over."

I don't want to go. What I really want is answers on who that woman is and why would she think she has claim over him. But now isn't the time. I know that. Not here, with twenty thousand witnesses. Instead of making a scene, I nod and Noel kisses my forehead.

"Ice. I mean it," he says as he steps away from me.

A collective sigh echoes around the arena and I suddenly want to puke. Can I deal with fighting women day in and day out over Noel?

This isn't me.

I am not the crazy girl that's willing to fight every woman in the world who looks at her man. What's wrong with me?

A couple security guards escort me off the stage and ask me if I'm alright.

"Sorry about that. Women. What can you do?" Noel says and the crowd laughs. I know he doesn't mean anything by it, but it stings a little. "Bet you guys didn't know you'd get two shows today."

The crowd laughs even harder and then the drums kick up the beat.

I want to die.

Back on the bus, I've managed to find a baggie and stuff it with ice. It stings when it touches my cheek, but the numb feeling on my skin is welcomed.

I can't even make it one day without making enemies. I plop down on the couch and close my eyes. This day can't possibly get any worse.

There's a knock on the outside door, just as I get comfortable. That's strange. I've never heard anyone knock on that door before. Most of the guys around here come and go as they please on this bus, but the show is still going strong so I know it can't be anyone associated with the band.

I don't think I can handle any more crazed fans today.

I shove myself up from the couch and twist the handle on the door. On the other side stands a very well put together Diana Swagger of Center Stage Marketing. Her red hair sits in a low bun against her neck and her pressed, tan suit flatters her curvy figure.

I look down at my torn black tank and jean shorts and panic surges through me. I'm a freaking disaster. I can only imagine what my hair and face look like.

Diana removes her *Gucci* sunglasses. "What the hell happened to you?"

I pull the ice pack away from my face and switch it to my left hand. My right hand rubs the moisture off on my shorts before I stick it out to greet her. "Hi, Ms. Swagger. Won't you come in?"

Diana raises an eyebrow and doesn't make a move to shake my hand. "You're a complete disaster."

She scrunches her nose while she digs her phone from her purse. I drop my hand down to my side. "Harold?

Yes. Hi. I found her. She's not..." She pauses and glances at me. "I'm not sure if this is going to work. You may need to come down here and get this account straightened out before we lose it completely."

Oh no. She's firing me already?

My heart leaps into my throat. If I don't work for her, there's no reason for me to stay on tour with Noel. "Please, wait. This isn't normally me. I wasn't expecting you this early. Please come in, give me a chance to explain. I'm begging you."

Diana stares at me but doesn't say a word. "Harold. I'll call you back." She ends her call and shoves her phone back in her purse. "Better be a damn good explanation."

Relief floods me as she brushes past me to step onto Big Bertha and I close the door after she's inside.

Diana looks around the bus. "You share this space with four men?"

I step around the counter and stand across from her. "It's not so bad. Noel and I share the bedroom in the back. The rest of the guys sleep in the foxholes."

Diana nods, but doesn't appear surprised by the news. "So you and Noel are an item?"

I tilt my head. "Well, yes. But you already knew that, right?"

"I had an idea." She adjusts the straps that rest on her shoulder to hold up her purse. "This explains his motivation to get you here," she mutters. "Typically we don't allow our employees to have personal relationships with our clients. This account with Black Falcon is rather large, and since Noel Falcon chose you personally, I have to let this slide. Just be warned, if Noel wants you gone, you'll be terminated. That is not up for negotiation."

I swallow hard. Lose my boyfriend and I lose my job. Those are some hefty stakes. "Understood."

Diana sighs. "Good. Now that we are the same page, let's go over a few things, shall we?" She sets her purse on the counter and pulls out an iPad. After a few clicks she sets it on the counter and turns it in my direction. "Here is your contract. H.R. conveniently forgot to go over it with you, which is why I got so lucky. It's standard, really. Basically, all it says is that you won't sell, trade, or disclose any marketing campaigns we are working on for any of our clients. It also has a non-compete clause."

"Non-compete?" I understood everything else other than that.

"That means if you leave or become terminated, you can't join a competing marketing firm within the state of New York."

I swallow hard. New York is the Mecca of advertising. Sure there are firms in other states, but my dream is a firm in New York. That's where all the action is and where I live with Aubrey. But this is my foot in the door. This is my shot. I have to take it. Noel and I will be fine, right?

"Where do I sign?" I ask.

Diana hands me a pen and has me sign the electronic document. Once I'm done, she turns the device towards her. "Let me just email this back to the main office and we'll get down to business."

We chat for the next thirty minutes about how I am expected to find out what the client, Noel wants and how he wants his charity represented. Apparently, he told them he wanted me to have complete creative control over the campaign.

My stomach twisted into a knot.

This is a lot of responsibility for a first job. I'm expecting to have help, but Diana makes it sound like I am on my own. If this falls apart, it will totally be my fault.

Diana checks her watch. "Any questions?"

Only a million, but none I can ask, without making myself look even more foolish to her than I already do. "No, Ma'am. I think you've made things quite clear."

She stands and straps her purse over her right shoulder. "If you have any questions, feel free to contact me." She hands me her business card, but I don't think she has sincerity about me calling her. "My car is waiting. I have a flight in an hour or so."

I raise my eyebrows. "They didn't allow you much time, did they?"

Diana cocks her head to the side. "If it'd been any other client, you would've only received a phone call from me, not a personal visit. That's how important this client is to my firm. Mr. Falcon's happiness means a great deal to me. So make sure he stays that way."

There it is again, the little jab that I only have my job because of Noel. Apparently my marketing degree from the University of Texas means nothing.

I follow Diana out of the bus and watch her get into a black Town car that waits for her beside the bus. She doesn't even look back, which confirms her pure loathing of me.

Great.

A shriek grabs my attention. A group of twenty or so female fans rush toward Noel as he makes his way toward the bus. He stops and takes a few quick pictures with the group along with autographing a few things before he glances at the bus. A shy wave is the best I can muster.

Noel waves back while security continues to hold the screaming girls back.

I step to the side and allow Noel past me onto the bus, once he breaks free from the crowd. "Hey." My voice is so timid I barely recognize it myself.

To make matters worse he doesn't say anything in return. This isn't going to be a good conversation.

I climb up the steps. Noel's hands grip the island countertop in Big Bertha's little kitchen—his full stature towering over it. He doesn't face me, but I don't need to see his face to tell he's angry with me.

"Noel, I'm really sorry if I embarrassed you or caused any trouble for you, but that girl, she—"

"She what, Lane?" Noel snaps and spins around to face me. "What could a fan possibly do to make you attack her at my show? I thought you were different. You're the mature one in this relationship, right?"

Tears brimmed in my eyes. "Noel, I'm sorry. I didn't mean for it to happen. The things she said made me snap. I know that's no excuse, but hearing another woman say she's going to sleep with you is just too much for me to handle. I acted before I even thought."

Noel sighs and threads his fingers into his sweaty hair. "Jealousy? That's what set you off? Jesus, Lane. Don't you know me at all? Why do you doubt my feelings for you? You always think you're second to me. No girl can ever compare to you."

I shake my head. "I never said that."

"You don't have to. Every time there's a choice to be made between you and something else in my life, you always think you'll be second. Four years ago on the dock, you left me because you said I would always choose music over you. That we'd never have a good life because you'd always come second. You told me that's why you were walking away because I wasn't thinking about you and the future. Today just proves you still think of me like that. That you aren't my everything."

Tears fall at the mere sound of his words. Is it always me who doesn't love him enough, not the other way around, like I've always believed? My shoulders shake as a sob escapes my throat.

Oh, God. I've ruined this.

This man, that I have all these feelings for, doesn't think I care about him enough. He has no clue that I love him with every ounce of my soul. I want him to trust me.

Noel wraps his arms around me. "Shhhhhhh. Lane, baby, I'm sorry. I didn't mean to make you cry. You just mean so much to me. The thought of you thinking you aren't my number one drives me crazy. Only you, Lane. You are all I'll ever want."

My fingers claw into his back as I cry harder and think the exact same thought.

Chapter 18

I sit on our bed and watch Noel pack an overnight bag for his trip out to Tucson. It's only for one night, but I just know that it'll feel like an eternity.

Noel zips up his bag and my heart sinks. It's time for him to go. "You got everything you need?" I ask and secretly wish he'll say he can't go, but then instantly feel guilt that I want to stop him from seeing a sick fan.

He stares down at me and licks his bottom lip. "Not everything."

A blush creeps over me. "Noel..."

He grabs my hand and pulls me to me feet. Every nerve in my body zings as he holds me tight against his chest. The things this man can do to me with a simple touch.

Noel's fingers trace the exposed skin on my lower back. "What do you say? One more time for the road?"

I giggle before his soft lips meet mine. "Your car is waiting and you'll miss your flight."

The thick muscles in his shoulders bunch under my hands as he shrugs. "I'll be really fast."

My fingers thread into the hair on the nape of his neck and Noel grins, knowing he's won this little battle. His hands knead my hips and urge them forward just as his lips attack mine. Fire burns hot in my core as I feel Noel's arousal press against me. His tongue flicks against mine and I hitch a leg around his hip.

Large hands cup my butt and lift me off the ground. Instantly, I wrap both legs around him and grind against him, wishing there weren't so many clothes between us. Noel spins around and plops down on the bed with me on his lap. He pops the button on my jean shorts and unzips them, exposing my thong.

A growl escapes him as he reaches inside my shorts and spreads his long fingers on my bottom. Noel pushes me forward, urging me to ride him with our clothes still on, while his tongue traces a line from my jaw to my collar bone.

Blue eyes smolder with desire as they look up to meet mine. "I want you so fucking much."

I lick my lips and yank his face to mine and Noel chuckles. He doesn't realize when he says things like that, I nearly lose my freaking mind.

His hands slide up my ribs as he takes off my tan top. Goosebumps erupt all over my skin when his fingers tease the curve of my breast. The need for his skin on my most intimate skin is almost unbearable. I shove my bra straps down and reach behind me to unclasp it.

Noel leans back and his eyes burn as they take in my every move—each one deliberately slow. The hook comes free with a twist of my wrist and I continue to slide the straps off and then discard the bra to the floor.

He licks his lips. "You are so damn beautiful."

Noel's lips crush into me and all I can think about is how much I want him. The thought of a night without him makes me savor this moment. Every inch of my world interweaves with this gorgeous man. It's amazing how attached I am in such a short time.

His fingers are magical as they trace the delicate skin under my waist band. I moan and squeeze him tighter in my arms and then run my fingers through the dark hair on the nape of his neck.

A loud knock on the bedroom door startles me and I lose my focus. I reluctantly pull away from Noel's lips and my shoulders slump. Noel sighs and rests his forehead against mine and lets out a string of soft curse words.

I giggle at Noel's frustration and kiss his lips knowing exactly how he feels.

The bedroom door flies open and I gasp. Riff barges through the door and his eyes land directly on my naked breasts. A shriek assaults my ears and it takes me a second to realize it came from me as I attempt to cover up my shirtless chest.

Noel protectively wraps his arms around me. "What the fuck, dude? I didn't say come in."

"Sorry, Bro. Didn't know you were..." Riff's eyes slide down my body and a slow grin spreads across his face. "...busy."

Noel's eyes narrow at Riff. "Well, now you know. So get the fuck out."

Riff glances at my horrified face and then turns his attention back to Noel. "Just thought you would want to know your ride to the airport has been waiting for almost twenty-five minutes, but I can see you're busy. I'll tell them to piss off."

A heavy sigh leaves Noel's mouth. "Thanks, man. Tell them I'll be out in a second."

Riff raises his eyebrows. "You sure? If I were you, I think I'd make them wait."

Noel's fingers roll into fists. "Yeah. Now get the fuck out."

The door closes behind Riff after he shrugs and mumbles something that sounds like "your loss" under his breath.

The tension in Noel's body lets up after Riff leaves the room. "I don't like how he looks at you."

I know exactly what he's talking about. Riff's gaze always seems to stay on me a few seconds too long, but I don't need to feed Noel's overactive imagination before he leaves. "He doesn't mean anything by it. Besides he and Aubrey have sort of a thing." I kiss Noel's neck. "My eyes and body are only for you."

He peers up at me through his long, sexy eyelashes. "Promise?"

I nod and place my lips on his.

"God, I wish you could come with me. I don't want to leave you."

"It's only for a night, Noel. How much trouble can I possibly get into?"

Noel wrinkles his nose. "With this bunch…a lot. Don't let them corrupt you while I'm gone, and don't listen to a damn word they say."

I laugh and kiss the tip of his scrunched nose. "You're adorable when you worry."

A smile creeps across his lips. "You think I'm adorable?"

"Quit fishing for compliments. You know the entire world thinks that about you."

"Fuck the entire world. All that matters is what you think of me."

I study his face. Does this man really need validation from me? He's Noel Falcon, for crying out loud. He shouldn't need me to validate anything, but after looking into his soulful eyes, I can see that he does. The look on his face tells me my opinion means everything to him right now.

The tips of my fingers trace the light stubble on his jaw line. "Of course I think you're adorable. You are irresistible and great in bed."

A sideways grin lights up his face before he threads his fingers into my hair. "That ride is going to have to wait after all."

I giggle as he flips me around and tosses me on his bed.

****

The bed is cold and lonely with Noel gone. The bus hums down the road at an even pace. The bumps in the road sound almost rhythmic as the tires roll along the asphalt. I toss back and forth. It's pointless to try and sleep.

The guys are playing music toward the front of the bus and their laughter is inviting. Four in the morning and they are still full of energy.

I sit up and shove myself off the bed. Light from the hallway streams into my eyes when I open the door—I squint to shield them.

"Hey, if it isn't sleeping beauty," Trip teases. "Lonely back there in the love shack?"

Heat creeps up my neck. These guys are never going to let me live down the fact they can hear Noel and I make love through the thin bus walls. I squeeze onto the small love seat beside Riff and try to avoid their stares. They hover around the small television, while Trip and Tyke battle in some shoot 'em up game.

"Lanie, since he isn't here, you have to tell us what Noel was like when you guys dated before," Trip says.

"Yeah," Tyke agrees, while adjusting the bandanna on his forehead. "We need dirt—the good stuff. Did he get the crap kicked out of him in school? We need ammo to torment him."

He always led a pretty drama free life. "Sorry, guys. There's isn't much to tell. Noel's pretty straight laced. He doesn't have many secrets."

"That *you* know of," Riff chimes in.

My head snaps toward him. "What's that suppose to mean? You keep alluding to some big thing Noel is keeping from me."

Riff shrugs. "It means just that."

"Noel doesn't keep things from me. He doesn't like secrets between us."

"Well maybe you should—"

"Dude!" Trip cuts Riff off. "Now is not the time, man."

"You don't think she should know? I guarantee he hasn't told her. Look at her face." Riff points to me. "She has no fucking clue what I'm talking about. I'm just trying to look out for her. She's a nice girl and I don't want to see her get hurt."

Trip rubs his forehead. "I know. I know. But, it's not our place to tell her."

I wave my hand. "Guys, I'm right here. Tell me what the fuck is going on."

Riff sets his eyes on me. There's a strange look on his face. It almost looks like pity. "Lanie...Noel has a girlfriend."

I furrow my brow. "What? No way! You guys are messing with me."

Tyke frowns at me, and Riff shakes his head.

"I—I don't believe you. He wouldn't...No."

Riff bites his lip, toying with the hoop through the bottom one. "It's true, Lanie. I'm sorry."

I clutch my chest. There's no air. I can't breath. I gasp, but it doesn't relieve the crushing weight in my lungs. *A girlfriend? What the fuck? Did I hear that right? Honesty? Truthfulness?* All lies. Everything out of Noel's mouth has been a lie. Having me here is all about sex. How can I be so naive to believe it's any thing other than that? He didn't give up until he got exactly what he wanted from me. My stomach rolls and my fingertips sting from clutching the couch cushion.

Things blink in black and white as my vision blurs. I feel lightheaded and a chill runs down my spine. I hear mumbles of voices from the guys, but I can't make out what they're saying. All I know is I'm losing it.

Tyke's on his knees in front of me, both hands on my shoulders. "Breathe, Lanie. You're white as snow."

I gulp down air into my lungs and focus on my breathing—in and out.

I'm going to kill that son-of-a-bitch.

How can he keep this from me? Why would he do this to me? I know I broke his heart once, but we were in high school. He knows I'm sorry for that. It was a stupid mistake. Do I really warrant such severe hurt?

Noel really is the womanizer the tabloids portray. The night we reconnected, I found him in a room with two half naked blondes. The thought of Noel breaking this poor girl's heart by sleeping with everything he sees makes me sick. There's no telling how many others there have been before me. "How long?"

"How long what, Lanie?" Tyke asks.

"The girl. Has he been with her long?" Tyke looks to Trip then Riff for an answer, which I find odd. It's almost like he needs permission to answer.

Riff rolls his lips into a line and I catch a glimpse of what almost looks like pain in his eyes. "Not long—only a few months."

"This whole time—why would he do this?"

"Because Noel Falcon is a selfish prick," Riff says. "He doesn't give a shit about anybody but himself."

I scrub my fingers down my face. My entire world crumbles before my eyes. "Oh, God. I can't believe this."

Riff's hand touches my shoulder gingerly. "I'm sorry, Lanie. He's a shit."

Tears sting my eyes and I pinch them shut. What am I going to do? My heart crushes in my chest as the weight of the situation bears down on me. Everything in my life centers on Noel and his band right now. Diana Swagger made it quite clear that I won't keep this job if Noel and I split.

Is this his plan? Crush me like I crushed him?

A wave of uncertainty ripples through me. How could I let this happen? How can I be so stupid?

The tears build up in my eyes and I don't want these guys to see me cry. I already look like a sad, pathetic, stupid fool to them. I don't want to add crybaby to the list.

My legs wobble as I push myself up from the chair. The urge to run as far away as I can hits hard.

"Lanie? Are you alright?" Tyke asks.

"I'm fine," I lie as I start towards the bedroom door.

It hurts to know I've been betrayed, but it feels worse to feel so naïve. I didn't see this coming. I trusted him.

I slam the bedroom door shut a little harder than I mean to after I pass through it. Tears fall uncontrollably once I'm alone and I allow a sob to escape me. This bedroom, once a place of happiness between Noel and I, now feels like a torture chamber.

Did he sleep with her on this bed—on these sheets? How many other women for that matter?

The thought disgusts me. Before I can stop myself I hurl myself at the bed, ripping and tearing at the sheets, while I cry. It takes less than thirty seconds for me to strip the mattress naked. The sheets lay in a massive heap in the corner of the small room.

I plop down hard on the bed and bury my face in my hands. What am I going to do? If I leave Noel's won and I can't let that happen. I need this job, and whether I like it or not he's the key to keeping it.

The need to hate him tears at me, and I want to hurt him. Hurt him like he's hurt me.

I stare at the sheets for long minute, then decide the best way to get to him is if I stay. Stay here and let him see how much I hate him. Stay here for the rest of the two weeks and show him he can't sabotage this job for me.

I debate on getting a match and setting the pile in the corner on fire. Instead, I grab the sheets from the floor and remake the bed. This is probably a stupid idea, but it's all I got. Noel will probably tell me to get the fuck out once he comes back and finds out the game is over—that he's been caught, but I don't care. I'll ignore him. The silent treatment is usually reserved for elementary school children, but I think this case calls for it.

A soft knock on the door startles me, and before I can say come in, it pushes open. Riff stands there in a wife beater t-shirt that fully displays his tattoos. His Mohawk reaches up at the ceiling in perfect alternating colors. My shoulders sag as I pat the spot beside me on the bed.

He gives me a sad smile and then obliges. "You okay?" I shake my head, but tell him yes. "That's not very convincing."

I sigh and feel the sting from crying in my throat. "I know, but what choice do I have?"

Riff tilts his head. "You have all the power here, Lanie. Noel screwed you over just like he did to me. That's just who he is. But you have the power to do what's best for you and get the hell away from him. I would if I could, but I'm kind of stuck here."

I snort. "I know the feeling."

"Ah, yes, the job—I almost forgot about that. Well, I guess you and I are both screwed by him."

I turn toward him. "You mean you'd leave this band if you could?"

Riff nods while keeping his brown eyes sets on me, like he's waiting for me to put the pieces of a puzzle together. "In a heart beat. I can hardly look at the guy without wanting to kick his ass. But, this band is my life. It's all I've ever known. I can't just walk away, no matter how much I want to."

"I've noticed there's some tension between you two."

Riff laughs, but it has a bitter edge to it. "Yeah, well, when your best friend fucks your woman, you'll have that."

My eyes widen. "Noel…"

"Yes," he answers my unspoken question. "His girlfriend is my ex, Sophie."

That's when I bolt to the bathroom before my guts spill all over the bedroom floor.

Chapter 19

Noel's flight lands at the Charlotte airport any minute. He'll be here soon and I don't have a fucking clue what I'm going to say to him. As much as I love the idea of using the silent treatment method, I don't think I'll be able to stop myself from lashing out at him at least once.

He needs to know I think he's a selfish bastard and I hate his guts.

The mouse on my laptop keeps sticking as I continue research into charities like Black Falcon's. I have to keep my mind busy somehow. If I allow it, my brain will drive me insane replaying thoughts of Noel and all the other women he's been with. I didn't insist he use a condom when we were together because stupid me, trusted him. Now, the thought of all the diseases I might now have makes me want to literally murder him.

I readjust myself in the bed and open a new search page. Mystery girlfriend has my mind curious. I tossed and turned all night wondering who she is and what she looks like.

I open a new search box and carefully type in, "Noel Falcon's girlfriend, Sophie," into the box before hitting send. It only takes a couple seconds for the results to pop up, but out of all the links, I don't see anything about Noel Falcon and a girlfriend.

I tap my finger on my chin and then it occurs to me I can still probably find this girl. I just need a different route. This time I type in, "Riff from Black Falcon's girlfriend, Sophie".

Bingo.

This time pages and pages of pictures flood my screen of Riff and a blonde named Sophie together. I click on a full length picture of her. As much as I hate to admit it, she's beautiful. Long, blonde hair cascades down her back and her legs are incredibly long, not to mention her perfect smile. I stare down at my very modest chest and then back to Sophie's.

We are exact opposites in every way.

Another thought occurs to me. I'm the other woman. Noel cheated on this gorgeous woman with me. That thought alone keeps me from hating her completely. It's not her fault Noel is a terrible person, but that doesn't erase the fact she came between two best friends.

She's still a fucking slut.

"What are you doing?"

My heart bangs against my ribs. Shit! He isn't supposed to be back yet.

I roll to my side and sit up after I slam the lid on my laptop shut. He stands there in his red t-shirt and distressed jeans looking like he hasn't slept much. Crazy rocker hair stands in place with a pair of black sunglasses resting on his head with both hands planted on his hips.

How dare he question my actions. "That should be my line."

Noel flinches. The look on his face gives him away. He knows I know.

He steps inside the room and shuts the door behind him. "Lane, you can't believe the shit you read on there."

I raise an eyebrow. "Oh, really. Who should I believe then, Noel? You?"

He takes two quick steps and sits on the bed next to me. He tries to wrap his arm around my waist, but I shove it off me. "Baby? Please. Let me explain."

I shake my head. "No. No more lies."

"I never lied to you."

"You're lying to me right now!" I shout. My entire body shakes, so much for being cool and blowing him off. "Were you ever going to tell me about Sophie? Or are your plans to revenge fuck me not complete yet?"

Noel grabs my chin between his thumb and index finger and forces me to look at him. "You're not just some piece of ass to me, Lane. How can you even think that?" My eyes water and I blink out a tear. It rolls down my cheek and Noel wipes it away with his thumb then cradles my face in his hands. "I love you."

A sob I can no longer hold back escapes me. "How can you love me when you have a girlfriend?"

His lips pull into a tight line. "It's complicated, but it's not what you think."

"Then tell me. Tell me why you would say things to me that make me believe I'm your world and not tell me you have someone else."

He sighs and rests his forehead against mine. "Because I can't leave her and I can't lose you."

I pull away from his hold and a cold chill runs through me. "Then why drag me into all this Noel? Why not let me work on the campaign from New York? You forced me to come here because you knew I still had feelings for you. You knew this would eventually happen and you have no intentions on leaving your girlfriend, and yet, you did it anyway. Riff is right. You are a selfish bastard."

"Riff? He's how you found out, isn't it? I'm going to fucking kill him!" He roars and bounces up off the bed.

"Noel!" I reach for him, but he flings the door open and storms down the hallway to Riff's foxhole before I have the chance to get out of bed.

Noel throws open the curtain and lunges inside. "You fucking told her?"

"You can't have them both," Riff yells back. "I won't let you do that to Sophie."

I jump off the bed. "Noel, stop!"

In a split second, Noel loses it. He yanks Riff from the bunk and throws him down on the hallway floor. Riff starts to stand, but before he gets the chance, Noel's on him, connecting a hard punch in his face.

Riff grunts and grabs Noel into a tight headlock. Noel flings his arms wildly, his fists cracking against Riff's ribs.

"Stop it!" I yell, while standing back. These two guys both have a good foot on me and at least sixty or so pounds. There's no way I can break them up without getting hurt.

Trip and Tyke's curtains fly back and they jump out of their bunks. The twins get in-between the two fighting men and pull them apart. Riff and Noel both still red-faced determined to get at each other.

"I can't believe you fucking told her!" Noel shouts while still in Trip's firm hold. "You need to mind your own damn business."

Riff laughs harshly. "Me? Mind my own business? You make it pretty hard to do when you're fucking my girlfriend behind my back!"

Noel's mouth drops open. "She came to me. I didn't go after her."

"And that makes it fucking okay? Jesus, Noel, you were my best friend—my brother and you still screwed me over. I'm not going to let you do that to Lanie."

"I was going to tell her!" Noel shouts with his arms spread wide.

"When? When were you going to tell her? After Sophie has the baby?"

I fall back against the wall. A baby? Did I just hear that right? Sophie's *pregnant*? With *Noel's* baby?

Noel's body stills and his eyes snap to mine. That's why he can't leave her. He fucking knocked her up. I shake my head. No. No fucking way this is happening to me. I am not this person. I don't get caught up in drama like this.

"Lane?" I hear Noel say my name as I continue to shake my head and back away from him. "Lane, wait!"

I turn on my heels and run back to the bedroom to grab my suitcase. I can't stay here. I can't stomach looking at him a second longer. The drawer flies open and I grab a handful of my clothes and throw them in the bag. It looks like a mangled mess, but a few wrinkles are the least of my problems.

The laptop on the bed goes in last and I zip up the suitcase. I freeze when I hear his voice. "Where are you going?"

Is he a complete idiot? Did he actually think I'd stay once I found out about Sophie? I shake my head and step around him into the bathroom to grab my make-up bag. The road with Noel isn't anything like I planned.

Noel grabs my arm as I pass back by him. "Aren't you going to talk to me?"

I yank from his grasp and head for the bed. "I have nothing to say to you."

He slams the door shut to our room. "Well, I have something to say to you."

I roll my eyes at him. Anything that comes out of his mouth will be a lie and I don't have time to listen to his bullshit.

I grab my suitcase. "Get out of my way, Noel."

"No. Damn it, Lane. You're going to listen to me, even if I have to tie you down to that fucking bed."

I narrow my eyes. "Wanna bet? Move."

"God damn it, Lane. Would you fucking stop and listen to me for two seconds." He runs his fingers through his hair. "I fucked up, alright. I know that. Sophie and I aren't what you think. Trust me. She means nothing to me."

I gasp. "You're worse than I thought, if you'd talk about the mother of your child like that. You really are an asshole, like your father."

His eyebrows shoot up. "I am nothing like that bastard."

"Oh no? I recall him turning his back on his child, too."

His jaw tightens and the muscle work beneath his skin. "What the hell do you know about being there for someone, Lane?"

That hurts. It's a direct blow to the heart. He's calling me out for leaving him four years ago and it can't come at the worst opportune time. Doesn't matter. Before I dumped his sorry ass, I was always there for him. "A hell of a lot more than you do, apparently."

"That's fucking bullshit. You turned your back on me. You always do. When you think I put something else ahead of you, you bail. You did it that night on the dock and you're doing it again now."

I shake my head. "That's not why I left you, Noel. I left you because you were a selfish bastard who cared more about himself than the person who loves you the most in the world."

The suitcase hits the floor with a loud thud when I yank it off the bed and roll it towards the door.

Noel steps in my path and grabs me by the shoulders. "Please." His voice is so low it's a near whisper. "Please stay with me."

I close my eyes. I can't look at him. Even though what he's done to me is completely shitty, I don't want to see him this way. Hurting him again is the last thing I want to do, but I can't stay. Not after all this. "Let me go, Noel."

"No," he says. "I'm going to fight for you. I need you to know you're my everything. I can't lose you again. I just want you to give me a chance, Lane—a chance to prove myself to you."

His words sting. How I wish they were true. If they were, he would've ended things with Sophie the minute we reconnected and told me everything. Instead, he hid everything from me.

"How can I trust you now?" I open my eyes and touch his cheek. "I'm sorry," I say before I step out of his hold and roll my suitcase out the door.

Chapter 20

This isn't the brightest idea I've ever had. I roll my suitcase through the parking lot and try to stay out of all the road crews way as they push and pull amps and speakers toward the arena. I'm not even sure what city we're in, let alone how to find a place to run away to in order to avoid running into Noel.

"Lanie?" I hear my name spoke by an unfamiliar voice and I turn. It's the bodyguard that's always herding Noel's fans away. Noel probably sent him to find me. Great.

"Oh, hey, Mike." I reply as coolly as I can and hope he doesn't notice the heavy-ass bag I'm toting around with me.

His eyes drop down on my hot-pink luggage. "You going somewhere?"

I tuck a loose strand of hair behind my ear. "Um, yeah, actually. I need to find a hotel, but I'm not sure how to get out of this place or even what city we're in, so I can Google a cab company."

He frowns at me. "I can take you if you want."

If he wasn't so big, I'd wrap my arms around him and thank him profusely for saving my life. "That would be awesome."

He smiles and for a second he loses that intimidating bear vibe and turns cuddly. "Come on, the Escalade is parked on the other side of the buses."

Mike takes over the handle of my suitcase and starts walking. I don't argue. With his muscles pulling that thing, we'll get out of here twice as fast.

When the SUV comes in sight he hits a button of the key and the trunk opens. Mike shoves my bag inside and we both jump in the cab.

"What hotel do you want to go to?" he asks.

I shrug. "It doesn't matter—the cheaper the better."

He nods and backs out of the parking space. "The tour manager booked us all rooms at a local hotel. You're more than welcome to have my room."

"Oh, no, Mike. I can't do that. You need your room."

He laughs and shakes his buzz cut head. "Lanie, you're welcome to it. I'll bunk up with one of the other guys. It's no big deal."

As bad as I feel for taking his room, I agree to it. Being broke majorly sucks in emergencies like this. What little money I have left in my checking account will be spent on buying me a plane ticket back to New York where I belong.

My heart instantly sinks. I don't belong there anymore either. Not only is my job at Center Stage Marketing flushed to hell, but that non-compete contract makes it impossible to get another marketing job in the city.

I'm royally screwed.

Mike pulls the Escalade under the awning of the Hilton and opens my door after he grabs my bag. "Come on. I'll check you in."

I smile. He's unbelievably nice. How can he work for a douche bag like Noel?

Mike walks up to the check-in desk and the blonde clerk blushes as she speaks with him. I can see why girls like him. He looks like he can lift you with one hand and plus has these amazingly cute dimples.

He grins, while the attractive blonde writes down what appears to be her number and slides it across the counter to him. He folds the little scrap of paper and tucks it, along with his I.D., back into his wallet.

Mike waves bye to the girl and then turns to me with the hotel key-card. "Room 211, Lanie. Do you need me to help you with your bag?"

I shake my head and pat his arm. "Thank you, but no. You've done so much to help me already."

The handle on my bag clicks as I pull it up.

Mike tilts his head and pulls his mouth into a tight line. "You know, Lanie, he's different with you. I've worked for him a long time and he's mentioned you several times before, but I didn't know how much he actually loves you, until he saw you again that first night in Houston."

I bite my lip. It's nice to hear confirmation of Noel's feelings for me, but it doesn't change the facts. "He's having a baby, Mike, and he neglected to tell me about it."

He frowns. "He has his reasons. All I'm saying is give him a chance to explain them to you. Maybe it's not what you think."

Before I can say anything else, Mike turns and heads for the exit. Noel's lucky to have him. That guy seems to really care about him.

It takes me two tries to get the room unlocked and get inside.

Stupid technology.

The room isn't anything special—a typical king-sized bed type room. I sit my bag on the floor and flop back onto the bed. What the fuck am I going to do? I scrub my hand down my face. This is one big clusterfuck.

My job is screwed.

My love life is shit.

I sigh and dig my cell phone out of my pocket and search Aubrey's number. "What's up lucky girl? How's that fine man of yours?"

I close my eyes. "Not good."

They're the only words I can get out before I start balling over the phone. I let it all go. The emotion and hurt I refused to let myself feel in front of Noel. Anger somehow put on the backburner as I allow my heart to break over the phone with my best friend.

"Aw, baby cakes, tell me what happened?" Aubrey sounds concerned.

It kills me to bring myself to admit to her what an awful person Noel is. "He's such an asshole."

She lets a heavy breath waft into the phone. "Did he hurt you? I'll kill him if he laid a finger on you."

I roll my eyes. "Nothing like that. He's just…" I take a deep breath. "Noel has a girlfriend, Aubrey."

"What!?" I rip the phone away from her shrill screech. "What do you mean he has a girlfriend?"

A tear rolls down my cheek and I wipe it away with the palm of my hand. It's hard to say that out loud. "I guess he has for a while, but that's not the worst part."

"What can be any worse than that?"

"She's pregnant."

Aubrey gasps. "Like, with a baby?"

I roll my eyes. "Yes. She says it's Noel's."

"Oh, my God. Screw the job, Lanie. Run away as fast as you can from that freak show. Come home."

I can't bring myself to tell her that Sophie is Riff's ex. That will only make her feel weird, and this situation is fucked up enough as it is, without adding that to the mix.

I sigh and think about catching the next flight back to New York, so I can wallow in my own apartment. Being anywhere around Noel Falcon is the last thing I want to do, which is why I'm here. To get some space and figure out what my next move is.

A knock on the door startles me. Damn, I should've put the do not disturb sign on the door since it's still midmorning. "Just a minute," I say.

"Who is that?" Aubrey questions.

I shove myself up from the bed and start towards the door. "It's probably just housekeeping."

I pull the door open, expecting to find maid service, and my heart clenches in my chest. "What are you doing here?"

Noel shrugs with his hands in shoved deep his pockets. The neck of his red shirt hangs lose from the fight with Riff and his dark hair still wild. His face red and the sparkle in his blue eyes gone, replaced by dullness. He looks awful. "Can I come in?"

A sane person would slam the door in his face after telling him to take a flying leap. As much as I want to do that, I can't bring myself to after looking at his face. He looks broken.

Maybe he actually cares that I left?

I pull the door open and he squeezes past me so I can shut the door. I lean my forehead against the door and take a deep breath. "Aubrey, I'll have to call you back."

"Is it him?"

I nod. "Yes."

She takes a breath. "Tell him to fuck off, Lanie. You don't need to put up with his shit."

After I tell her okay, and she's satisfied I'm about to throw him out on his ass, I end my call. He's waiting in silence—waiting on me to make a move. Since I've already let him in, I have no choice but to face him—to hear him out.

I turn around and lean against the door, but I can't look at him. The worn carpet on the floor marks a path from the bed to the door. It makes me wonder how many happy couples spent romantic weekends in this room and if any ever went through anything like this situation—betrayal by a lover.

Noel takes a step toward me and grabs my hand. I try to jerk away but he refuses to let go. "I know you hate me and never want to see me again, but I can't let that happen. You mean everything to me, Lane. I don't love Sophie. I never have, but I love you, more now than ever. I can't lose you."

My chest crunches tight at the sound of her name on his lips. A tear falls from my eye. "Why did you sleep with her, Noel? How could you betray Riff like that? More importantly, how could you keep this from me? We are not supposed to have secrets."

He sighs and then brings my knuckles to his lips. "I don't even remember her getting into my bed, to tell you the truth. I'm not always on my best behavior and, honestly, I was too wasted most of the time to remember much of anything, a few months ago. One morning, I woke up and there she was—completely fucking naked. I knew Riff would go through the fucking roof when Sophie told him what happened, so I bought her a plane ticket home."

"You sent her home?"

He nods. "I wanted the problem gone. I felt like shit because I couldn't believe that even in a fucked up state I could let that happen. Riff's the only family I have. I would never dick him over like that, or so I thought. That's why I sent her away—to fix things."

"You don't remember sleeping with Sophie at all?"

Noel frowns. "Nothing. That's what kills me. I watched Riff call her a million times after he figured out she split, knowing at some point I would have to fess up to my shit. To be honest, I prayed Sophie would never tell him, but I knew she would. It's just the kind of person she is." He takes a ragged breath and pinches the bridge of his nose. "She told him we'd slept together, and she could never go back with him after that."

I shake my head. Poor Riff.

"Riff immediately hated me—despised me for taking her away from him. We've fought so many goddamn times over her, I've lost count. I try to explain to him that I don't love her, but he won't listen. That only makes things worse. He'll never forgive me."

"Have you seen her since she left?"

He shakes his head. "No, and I never planned to either, not until a month ago when she called Riff to tell him she's pregnant with my baby. I have a hard time wrapping my head around it, you know. Even wasted, I always use a condom when I sleep with someone. I don't know how this happened to me."

I look into his eyes. "You didn't use a condom with me."

Noel's gaze flick to mine. "That's because you're you, Lane. I love you. You're the only girl I've ever loved and I had to fucking have you. I had to be near you—feel you completely. I've missed you so much."

I blink out a couple more tears. "If you haven't seen her, why do people call her your girlfriend?"

He sighs and then pinches his nose between his thumb and forefinger again. "I called Sophie after I found out she was pregnant. She told me she's almost positive it's mine and I felt sick. I always thought when I start a family it will be with the love of my life. Someone just like you." My stomach knots and my legs feel week. I grip the door handle for support. "The thought of a little kid running around out there that belongs to me makes me want to step up to the plate. I don't want the kid to hate me. If Sophie's baby is mine, I want to be there for it."

Noel will make a great father and I guess I didn't give him enough credit. He's not as immature as I thought.

I shake my head. "That still doesn't explain the whole girlfriend thing."

He shrugs. "Sophie said the only way she'll let me be a part of the whole process is if she can claim we're together—something about not wanting to look like a slut and all that."

"But you're not even sure the baby belongs to you."

"I know, but if it is, I want to be a better father than mine is to me. I want to be in its life. I won't turn my back on it. If Sophie wants to call herself my girlfriend so I can, that's fine, but I don't have to love her and it doesn't have to be true."

"Do you know how absurd that sounds?"

Noel nods and his sets gaze on me. "I would've never agreed to it, Lane, if I knew that we were going to happen. You have to believe me."

Mistakes can happen. I know this. I know Noel isn't a virginal type of guy. Hell the whole world knows he has a massive sexual history, but the world also doesn't get to see this sweet side of him—the side that will do anything for anyone. My Noel.

"Can't you just wait and get paternity tests once the baby's born then take her to court for visitation? I'm pretty sure you can afford an attorney.

"I could do that, but then I'd miss all the ultrasounds and the birth. I want to be apart of everything, if that's my kid."

"If the baby isn't yours, then that means it's…"

He rubs his face. "Not Riff's. He can't have kids. He got into some kind of accident when he was younger or something."

"But, it's possible, right? She was with him before you."

The thought of Riff and Noel sharing the same girl makes me shudder.

"I don't think so."

"How does Riff feel about all this?"

Noel shrugs. "He won't talk to me about it. He feels betrayed and won't speak to me. Whenever I try to talk to him about it, things get…ugly, and that's not good for the band."

He's right. This whole situation sucks, especially for the band. I've seen the tension between the two, in action myself. I knew all that male territory marking was about more than just me.

Noel drops my hand and then runs his fingers through his hair. His hands stay behind his head while he paces near the foot of the bed. I've never seen him like this before—torn between wanting me and needing to take responsibility for a fucked up mess.

I can't watch him fall apart like this. It's not him. "Would you stop that? You're making me nervous."

He stops and sighs, before sitting on the edge of the bed. Both of his shoulders slump as his blue jeans strain against the length of his long, muscular legs. My eyes roam over his body. His chest heaves under his red t-shirt as he rests his elbows on his knees and stares at the ground.

I can't help but think this is one of the last times I'll be locked alone in a room with Noel Falcon. This somehow feels like our goodbye. The accusation of always leaving because I'm second to him plays out, yet again. There's no way I can stay with him while he's caught up in all this baby-mama drama.

A few quick steps and I find myself next to him. My body seems to have a mind of its own when it comes to Noel. The pull to him is crazy. I sit down next to him on the bed. Our hips and legs touch and I lift my hand hesitantly to rub his back. As much as I wish this wasn't happening, he's still one of my oldest friends and he's hurting.

He sighs and reaches over and grabs my other hand, bringing my wrist to his lips and kissing the delicate skin over my pulse point. Need zings through me and I squeeze my thighs tightly.

"Thank you," he whispers against my skin. "Thank you for staying with me."

My lips turn down into a frown. He doesn't know this is my goodbye to him. "Noel..,"

He brushes my lips with his fingertips. "Shhhhhh. Let's not talk about this anymore. I just need to hear you say you love me. That this isn't going to ruin us."

I bite my bottom lip. Even though I'm unbelievably pissed at him, I can't deny the feelings in my heart. I do love him, more than anything else, but I can't do this. I can't be the other woman.

Noel's eyes plead with me to tell him I love him, and that I still need him.

I pull his fingers away from my lips and then bring both of my hands around to cup his face. He turns his head and kisses the palm of my hand. One last kiss is all I can bring myself to give him. I can't tell him that I love him, even though I do madly, it will only lead him on.

Every line and curve of his face I commit to memory. Never again will I hold him like this.

I lean and press my lips to his and he shuts his eyes. He tenses and tentatively moves his lips with mine. A single tear rolls down his cheek. He feels it too. He knows me well enough to know, this is it for us.

Noel wraps his arm around my waist and pulls me into him. Panic surges through me. If he starts touching me, it'll be over. It doesn't take much from him to turn me on, and I know I can't let my body overrule my head.

I break our kiss and lean my forehead against his. "Noel...I can't."

He opens his eyes. "Can't or won't?"

I shrug and drop my hands into my lap. "Does it really matter?"

"It matters to me, Lane. We can work this out. I just need some time to—"

I shake my head. "No, Noel. I can't be that girl. I can't be the girl who is second in your life. You've always known this about me. I can't believe you didn't tell me."

He lays his hand on my thigh and my whole body tingles. "Would you've come here—been with me, if you'd have known? I wanted you here—with me—and when I saw my shot to make that happen, I took it."

I cross my legs in attempt to create more space between us, but my body instinctively turns into him. "But you lied to me. I can't forgive that."

A harsh breath escapes his lips. "I didn't mean to hurt you, Lane."

I move his hand off my thigh. "I believe you, but that doesn't change the situation. I understand you feel like you need to be with Sophie. I do. But I can't be a part of your life during all this."

Noel tilts his head. "What are you saying?"

I take a deep breath. "I need you to leave."

"Lane?"

I shake my head and close my eyes. "Please leave."

"No. Don't say that. Don't shut me out."

He's not going to go willingly, and if I don't end this now I might let him con me into staying with him, being second in his life. I gaze into his eyes try to look as hard as possible. "Noel, I'm done with you."

He grabs my hand, and I jerk away from his grasp. "No."

I shove myself off the bed. "Get the fuck out."

Noel stands and steps in front of me. He leans into me, and I take a step back, bumping against the wall behind me. "You want me to go?"

"Yes."

His eyes search my face while his warm breath hits my lips. Each of his hands goes on either side of me, effectively pinning me against the wall. Our thighs touch as he pushes against me. I swallow hard and try not to think about how close his body is to mine. His nose traces runs along my chin. "Are you sure?"

"Yes."

Noel kisses my chin, and I close my eyes. My head tips back. His lips feel amazing and my chest actually heaves. "You can really give this up? Won't you miss how I make you feel?"

Of course I'll miss this. The entire time we were apart I missed him. This time won't be an exception, but for my own sanity, I have to end this. I can't allow my feelings to be toyed with. It scares me to know I've fallen for him again so quickly. If I allow this thing between us to continue and he eventually leaves me for Sophie, I'll be crushed.

I'm just trying to think ahead.

A tear rolls down my cheek, and I turn my head away from him. "Please stop hurting me." The words only come out as a whisper, but I know he hears them.

He flinches, drops his arms—freeing me from his muscular prison and takes a step back. He runs his hand roughly through his hair. "I'm sorry, Lane."

Before another word can be said between us, he turns on his heel and heads out the door. I jump when the door slams behind him.

Chapter 21

The cheapest flight to New York leaves tonight at nine o'clock. It sucks I have to pack up and leave this room Mike so graciously gave to me for free. Check out is noon and hanging out in the airport for eight hours will suck so much.

I throw my pajamas in my bag and zip it up.

I walk toward the door just as a knock startles me. I open the door without looking through the peephole and stop in my tracks. "Mike? What's up?"

He shoves his sunglasses on top of his head. "Oh, good. You're ready."

I tilt my head. "Ready?"

"Yeah, I'm here to take you back to the bus."

I shake my head. "I'm sorry you wasted your time coming over here, but I'm not going back."

Mike frowns and his eyes look sad. "Noel knew you would say that. Here." He hands me a paper.

I take it from him. "What's this?"

"Your contract."

My brow furrows as I read through the very legal document that bares my signature and Noel's on the bottom. "I don't understand."

Mike shrugs. "It basically says if you don't follow through with seeing this charity project through Black Falcon can sue you."

"Me?" I nearly shriek. "He wouldn't…"

"I think you underestimate how far Noel will go to get his way."

That selfish son-of-a-bitch. Sue me? Is he seriously stooping to this level? I'm going to kill him. I rub my face as my pulse races under my skin. "Where is he? The bus?"

Mike nods and grabs my suitcase. "Come on, I have the Escalade parked out front."

After we get settled into the SUV and get on the road, I notice Mike glances at me every couple of seconds. His concern is sweet and I appreciate it, but right now I'm too pissed to even speak without yelling. I map out in my mind exactly what I'm going to say to Noel. Every vulgar curse word I know pops into my head at least once. I can't believe he has the nerve to pull this shit.

Mike parks near Big Bertha and shuts the engine off. "Take it easy on the guy, Lanie. He's desperate to keep you around."

I pick at my nail to keep from looking at Mike's face. He works for Black Falcon, so of course he's going to take Noel's side. "Thanks for the ride, Mike. I hope this won't take too long. There's a flight back to New York tonight with my name on it."

He chuckles. "I won't hold my breath. Noel usually gets what he wants."

I roll my eyes as I open the door. "So I've heard."

Mike beats me to the back of the SUV and hands over my luggage. "See you around."

More than anything, I want to laugh and bet him he'll be surprised with just how little Noel will get his way with me, but I don't. I don't want to sound bitter and childish. Instead, I wave to him and pop the handle on my suitcase.

Trip and Tyke open the door to the bus and step out onto the pavement. Trip notices me and elbows Tyke. They both stand there waiting for me to approach. This could be bad. It looks like they want to guard the door and not let me on.

I tilt up my chin when I'm within a couple feet from them. I'm getting on that bus to give Noel Falcon a piece of my mind and those two aren't going to stop me. "Hey, guys. Noel in there?"

Trip grins. "Nice! You're still coming with us. This should be interesting."

I shake my head. "I just have some...business with Noel."

Tyke looks concerned while Trip appears absolutely delighted.

I run my fingers through my hair and start towards the door. Tyke places a hand tentatively on my forearm. "Are you sure you want to do that, Lanie?"

I stop and tilt my chin up. "I appreciate your concern, Tyke, but I can handle Noel."

He removes his hand and nods before patting his brother on the back. "Come on, bro. Riff's not in there, so I think it's safe to let her in."

They part and Trip motions me by with a grand sweep of his arm.

I fling open the door and my suitcase bangs against each step as I make my way up. Noel's sitting on the edge of one of the captain's seats strumming his guitar. He doesn't even bother to help me with my bag as I lug it inside.

Jerk.

I fold my arms and stand there, ready for a fight, but he just keeps playing that stupid guitar like I'm not even there. He closes his eyes and hums to the melody like he's trying to figure out the lyrics. I remember him doing this very same thing when we dated before. Noel licks his lips and then slides the bottom one between his teeth. It's a simple move, but it's unbelievably sexy. The need to feel his skin on mine causes my pulse to kick up a notch.

Damn him. He's doing this to me on purpose.

I reach over and wrap my fingers around the neck of his guitar, cutting off its sound. Noel opens his blue eyes and grins in that sexy way that makes me weak in the knees. "Oh, hey, Lane, I didn't see you there. You can go ahead and take your stuff on back to the bedroom."

Is he serious right now? "Do you think this is some kind of game, Noel?"

He rests his arms causally on the guitar—tattoos directly in my line of site—fully on display. "I don't know what you're talking about. I'm simply directing a guest, slash employee, where to store her personal belongings. Don't see much of a game in that."

I throw my arms up. "You're unbelievable! You know that? If you think for one minute that you can force me to stay here, you've—"

In one swift move, Noel leans the guitar against the wall and stands directly in front of me. Damn these tight—

spaced buses. He reaches down and grabs my bag. I try to swat away his hands, but he's too quick.

I stay hot on his heels as he starts down the hallway. "Give me back my stuff."

"No," he says before he unzips the suitcase, takes two more steps, and then dumps all the contents on the bed.

The clothes, make-up, and other personal items land in a messy heap on the bed. "You asshole! Why did you do that?"

His eyes meet mine. "Because the sooner you see you aren't going anywhere the better."

I snatch the clothing into my arms. Noel smirks at me as he shoves my bag behind his back. I scowl at him. "What's your problem? Give it to me."

A loud thud sounds in the tiny room as Noel drops the luggage behind him. "Keep being so bossy with, me and I might just give it to you right now." He wiggles his eyebrows suggestively.

I roll my eyes. "You're crazy. I can't keep up with you and these Dr. Jekyll/Mr. Hyde mood swings you've got going on."

He steps so close to me his leg touches mine. "No mood swings, Lane. I'm just making sure you keep your end of the deal."

"How can you expect me to stay here after all this?" I whisper.

Noel grabs the waistband of my jeans and yanks me flush against him. Heat sears through me as he dips his index finger inside my jeans and traces the sensitive skin on my stomach. I squeeze my eyes shut and feel my head tilt back. Damn my stupid body for wanting him.

He chuckles, and my eyes land on his smug face. "See how easy I can turn you on? That's why I expect you to stay—because you still want this."

He releases me, and I gasp at the loss of his warmth which makes him smile even bigger. Why does he have to be so damn sexy? It makes the inner battle between my body and my head unwinnable.

I hug my clothes tight against my chest as Noel steps around me without another word and heads out the door—so much for having a rational conversation with him.

The contract I signed with Center Stage Marketing lies on the bed. It obviously fell out of my bag when Noel decided to dump all of its contents out.

I lay my stuff on the bed and sit down next to the contract. Legal stuff wasn't my strong suit in college, but I pick it up and read down through it. It all looked pretty standard except for the last few clauses. One said that if I didn't fulfill my personal obligation of remaining on tour with Black Falcon for the full two weeks, I put myself at risk for being sued by the band for breach of contract by both Black Falcon and Center Stage. Diana conveniently forgot that little gem of information when she was explaining this.

I'm not even sure that's legal, but I did sign it along with Noel and Diana, and I've watched enough corny judge television shows to know a signed contract means a lot in court.

The second point says, at the end of the tour, Black Falcon will hand over all rights to the band to Center Stage.

That's when it occurs to me why Diana brought this contract to me personally. It isn't exactly on the up and up, and she probably doesn't want anyone else in the firm knowing about her dirty little deal with Noel to make me stay here.

Anger boils through me that both of these people trapped me here to get what they want.

I sigh, then fold the paper up and stuff it into my back pocket. A new found determination pumps through me to show both of them how great at selling myself, I can be. Since they seem to be able to hold me here legally, I'm going to have to suck it up and figure out a way to be around Noel, without letting him crush my heart.

Chapter 22

I don't bother watching Black Falcon's concert tonight. The further I stay away from Noel, the better. Besides, I've gotten a ton of work done on the literacy charity holed up in this bedroom all day. And it's fine by me if he stays away from me.

My phone buzzes next to me on the bed.

Aubrey.

She's been texting me like crazy since I our phone conversation this morning. I'm not even sure who she hates more at this point—Diana or Noel. Both of them, to her, are the scum of the earth now, though.

Are you sure you don't want to say screw 'em and come home anyway. You can reschedule your flight.

I look at the clock on my laptop. My flight already left, and if it wasn't for this piece of paper in my back pocket that can possibly ruin my life if I'd left now, I would. I would hop on an airplane back to New York and not bat an eye.

I sigh and text her back. *I'm stuck.* ☹

A hoot from the front of the bus draws my attention. The guys must be back. Several voices fill the bus, and Trip's stands out over all the rest.

"Hell of a show, guys! Did you see that crowd when Noel sang the encore? They were intense. One of the best gigs we've played all year. I say we get fucked up to celebrate!"

I tense at the mention of Noel's name. He's going to come back here again and try to get under my skin. To prove how much I still want him.

The thought both terrifies me and intrigues me. On one hand, I want him so badly it hurts. The last couple days we spent together were amazing. The mere thought of his hand sliding down my body causes me to erupt with goosebumps. But on the other hand, he has a fucking girlfriend, whether he claims her or not. A very pregnant girlfriend who claims he's the baby's dad.

He says he wants to be with me, but those are just words. Even through his own admission he won't leave Sophie to be with me. So where does that put me? Am I a play toy to be discarded when he's done with me?

I shake my head. That's exactly why I need to keep my distance from him. I can't let that happen.

I hear a couple cans open, which I assume are beer, before Trip says, "All right boys, there's a hot piece of ass waiting for me outside the bus. I got to get to it."

"How hot?" Tyke asks.

"Fucking ten, dude," Trip replies.

"She got a hot friend?"

Trip laughs. "Come on, little brother, I'm sure we can find you a score."

I listen as the twins head off the bus bickering about which one is actually older, when my stomach rumbles. I don't know what it is about this damn bus that makes me to forget to eat. Noel or not, I have to find food out there.

I save the work on the project and shut my laptop before I shove myself off the bed. My bare feet pad down the hallway and into the kitchen. Riff leans against the island with a package of Oreos in front of him. He pours milk into a red plastic cup on the counter and then recaps the jug.

He glances up and gives me a sad smile. "Hey. You want some?"

I shrug after I look around and find no sign of Noel. "Sure."

Riff turns and grabs another cup from the cabinet. "I'm surprised to see you. I figured you'd be in New York with Aubrey by now."

Obviously, Riff doesn't know about the contract. I should tell him. Let him know about yet another underhanded thing Noel Falcon has done to a woman, but I decide against it. This band is struggling without any help from me. It doesn't take a genius to figure that out after what I saw yesterday.

"Trust me. I wish I was."

He pushes the package over to me as he pours me a cup of milk. "Want to talk about it?"

I shake my head. Riff is already fully aware of my plight. No need to rehash it. "Thanks for the milk…and the cookies."

"No problem." Riff smiles as he tilts his head, almost like he's studying me. "You know, I meant what I said the other day. We should be friends. You can talk to me. Noel will never find out."

I dunk my cookie in the milk and avoid his stare. "I'll keep that in mind."

The last thing I need is another close relationship with a member of Black Falcon. His offer seems innocent enough, but I can't shake the feeling that winning me over to his side is a competitive thing with Noel.

What's with these two going after each other's girls?

Uncomfortable with where this conversation may go, I grab a couple more cookies to take to the bedroom. "Thanks for these and the...talk."

Riff touches my shoulder. "No problem, Lanie. Anytime."

Once I close myself inside the room, I plop back down on the bed and get back to work. It's the easiest way to distract myself from thinking about Noel.

After a couple hours of good solid work, I glance at the clock. It's after midnight, and the bus is still quiet. I heard Riff leave shortly after our run-in, and found comfort in being completely alone on this bus.

My vision blurs as I fight to keep my eyes open. I didn't sleep for shit last night and suddenly the bed is very appealing. The lights flick off with the flip of a switch and I snuggle down into the blankets.

I'm nearly asleep when the door flies open, and a drunken Noel staggers into the room. He makes his way over to his side of the bed and laughs when he bumps his knee in the process.

"Noel?"

Before I can even ask what he's doing, he makes it painfully clear when he wrestles his black shirt over his head. Light streams in from the hallway, allowing a beautiful display of his chest in front of me. I stop myself at that thought. I shouldn't be thinking of him that way. He doesn't belong to me. He's Sophie's. Noel told me that himself.

"What are you doing?" I whisper harshly. "Put your shirt back on."

Noel laughs as he unbuttons his jeans. I turn my head away as his cock springs free. "Damn it," he mutters, at the same time I think he should really invest in some underwear. "Look what you did, Lane."

What I did? *Excuse me*? I haven't done a thing to you."

He chuckles as he nearly falls over while taking off his boots and jeans. "Yeah, well, that's the problem. I have this raging hard-on whenever you're around and now you refuse to play with me anymore."

I cover my eyes to avoid nude Noel standing beside the bed. "Well, get used to it. That's never happening again." I risk a glance at his perfectly hard body and then immediately cover my eyes again. "Ugh. Would you please put your clothes back on and get the hell out of here?"

He ignores me and crawls under the covers. "Where am I supposed to go, huh? Tell me that."

I fold my arms over my chest. "Not my problem. Now, get out."

He snuggles further down into the pillow. "No can do. Get used to it, babe. You and I are roomies for the next couple days."

Noel reaches around my waist and pulls me into his body. Hard liquor lingers on his skin and a distinct smell of women's perfume. I pry his fingers off my hip, and he sighs deeply and closes his eyes before he rolls over.

I stare at the large cross tattoo etched into his back. Where does he get off thinking he can come in here and crawl into bed with me after what he's done?

A soft snore accompanies his chest rising and falling slowly. He's passed out—so much for forcing him to leave.

I grunt, frustrated and flip over to my other side. This is going to be a very long two days.

Chapter 23

The annoying ring tone for my mother sings through the air. I peel my eyes open and instantly freeze when I discover a very naked Noel Falcon wrapped around me. His tattooed forearm rests across the bare skin on my stomach. I attempt to lift it off me, but Noel bats my fingers away and reattaches himself to me.

"Stop, Lane. I'm trying to sleep," he grumbles with his eyes shut.

I ignore him and shove his hand off, not caring this time if it woke him or pissed him off. When I fling my legs over the side of the bed, two large hands wrap around me and slide me back into bed. Noel rolls on top of me, effectively pinning me to the bed.

The phone stops ringing, and I push on his chest, which he seems unfazed by. He traces my cheek with the pads of his fingers and my toes curl with such an intimate touch. Blue eyes gaze straight into mine before flitting down to my lips.

My heart hammers with the anticipation of him kissing me.

Noel tips his head down and our noses touch. "Since you seem to be up early, there's somewhere I want to take you."

My shoulders slump against the mattress. That isn't what I thought he was going to ask for.

Noel notices my disappointment and chuckles. "Don't get me wrong. I won't object if you want to stay in bed with me all day."

I frown. "Just because I didn't throw your drunk ass out of here last night doesn't mean I've changed my mind about being with you."

He shrugs. "Maybe…maybe not. I don't think it'll take much to wear you down and see my side of this situation."

I shake my head. "That's where you're wrong. I'll never be the other woman, Noel."

"You're not. You're *the* woman."

I open my mouth to protest, but before I get the chance Noel rolls away from me and hops off the bed. He grabs a towel from the cabinet and wraps it around his still naked waist before heading to the bathroom. "Hurry up and get ready. I want to spend the day with you."

I rake my hands through my hair and take a deep breath. He still doesn't get that we're over…again. I roll over and pick up my phone and send Mom a quick text that I would call her a little later.

A few minutes later, Noel returns from his shower, wearing only a towel. He doesn't hesitate when he drops it to the ground and pulls a clean pair of jeans out of the drawer.

Noel frowns. "You aren't dressed."

"That's because I'm not going anywhere with you."

He tugs on my hand, and I snatch it away from him. "Come on, Lane. Can't we get through this?"

I sigh and rub my forehead. "Are you still drunk? No. No, we can't get through this. You're having a baby with someone else."

"But—"

"No fucking buts, Noel. We're done. From this point on this—" I gesture between him and I. "—is just a business relationship."

He shakes his head and closes his eyes. "It doesn't have to be that way."

"Yes, it does. I'm basically a prisoner here. Between you and Diana, you've made it impossible for me to get out of this deal without ruining my financial future."

"Lane…"

I hold up my hand. "Just stop talking. I don't want to hear another word out of your mouth."

Noel pulls his lips into a tight line. The muscle in his jaw works visibly under his skin. "Fine. Fuck it. If you say we're done, then we're done."

I open my mouth to tell him not to be like that, but quickly shut it. He's right. We are done. How can we possibly work anything out? He belongs to someone else.

When he sees I'm not going to argue with him, he yanks a shirt out of the closet, and slams the door behind him as he leaves.

I rub my forehead and sigh. This sucks so much. It's not supposed to be like this. How can he pretend like things aren't completely fucked up? I mean, he wouldn't have anything to do with me if I were pregnant by another guy and refused to leave him. Why does he expect any different from me?

****

Out of sheer boredom, I attend the Black Falcon show. If I have to spend one more moment cooped up in that stupid bus, I will go nuts.

Embrace the Darkness rocks the crowd. Striker's long hair flings around as he bangs his head to the beat. He flips his head up and points to the people in front of him as he belts the chorus. The entire place sings along with him and he holds his microphone out to them. Even I know every word to this song. It's number one on the charts right now.

The song ends, and Striker pumps his fist in the air one last time. Screams for the band fill my ears, and I smile as they saunter off the stage one by one.

"Great set, guys," I tell the members of the group as they pass by me.

Striker grins as he nears me. "Lanie, love, great to see you again."

I smile as his eyes roam over my face. "You too."

He peers over my shoulder, and I turn to follow his eye line. Noel strides through a circle of adoring fans, but stops dead in his tracks when he spots me and Striker. He narrows his eyes, and for a second it appears that he might charge at us and read me the riot act for talking with Striker, but he doesn't. Instead, he turns in the opposite direction.

"An odd fellow, that one," Striker says. "He wants his hooks in you, that's for sure."

I face him. "Well, that isn't going to happen."

His eyes light up, and a broad smile covers his face. "There's an after party for the bands. You ought to go."

I swallow hard. This feels a little soon, but it will be a good distraction from everything that's going on.

Striker tucks a lock on his dark hair behind his ear, and I can't help but notice that he's pretty damn attractive.

I stare into his chocolate eyes and nod. "Yeah, absolutely."

"Great! I'll be watching for you." He touches my shoulder lightly as he steps around me.

Out of nowhere, Noel appears beside me the instant Striker is gone. "What did he want?"

I shrug. "To talk."

Trip and Tyke take the stage and the crowd starts to go crazy. I watch the two men tease the crowd with waves and a couple quick notes from their instruments and do my best not to look at Noel. The weight of his stare on my face tries to force me to look at him.

Riff steps up next to the stage and yells, "Noel! Come on, man, let's do this!"

"In a minute," he answers. "Lane?"

I shut my eyes and try to pretend he isn't talking to me.

He grabs my elbow and twists me toward him. "Look at me."

His bright-blue eyes waver with a sad look and it hurts me to see him this way. I sigh and try to look away to keep the emotion that's welling inside me.

Noel takes my chin between his fingers and forces me to see him. "Don't promise Striker anything. You're going to be mine again, one day."

My heart bangs against my ribs. The intensity of his eyes and voice sends shivers through me. He's so sure that we're getting back together, and it's a little overwhelming.

"Noel! Man hurry up!" Riff shouts, impatience thick in his voice.

Noel opens his mouth to say something, but takes another look at me, and quickly closes it. He leans in and kisses my forehead before he turns toward the stage.

Throughout the show, Noel glances in my direction, almost like he's double checking that I'm still there. When it's time for Black Falcon to perform their hit ballad, he sits on a stool and turns in my direction. He brings the mic up to his lips and sings soft words about being in love.

I bite my lip under the scrutiny of his stare, and he smiles at me.

He's basically serenading me before a crowd full of strangers and it's intense. The intent of his feelings is apparent, even Riff notices, but Noel continues to sing to me. A couple of off notes from the lead guitar catches my attention, and I watch as Riff steps directly into Noel's view of me.

Noel hops off the stool and tries to step around Riff, but it doesn't work. Riff blocks every step he takes. It obviously pisses Riff off that Noel is doing this to his ex.

Noel tries again, and Riff stops playing and shoves Noel's shoulder. Sensing the impending fight, I decide it's best if I get out of Noel's eyesight before we have a very public brawl in the middle of their set.

I turn away and book down the steps leading off the stage. Noel calls my name over the microphone, but I don't bother turning back. The sooner he learns to let this relationship go the better things will be for everyone involved.

Chapter 24

I catch a ride to the after party with Trip and Tyke before Noel gets an opportunity to tell me about how awful of a guy Striker is or something. A bodyguard I'd never seen before rides along with us. Mike is usually the one that hangs out with Noel and I, so I'm getting kind of used to him.

Squeezing between the two twins, I wonder how long the ride to the club is.

"What made you want to party with us?" Trip asks.

"Not that we're complaining or anything," Tyke throws in.

I shrug and smile at them both. "Just needed to get out."

Trip grins. "Yeah, right. You sure it doesn't have anything to do with Striker?"

My mouth hangs open. "How did you—"

Trip laughs. "What? Know the lead singer of Embrace the Darkness has a thing for you?"

"Yeah."

"Noel won't shut up about it. He's been bitching the entire time."

I square my shoulders. "Why should he care? He has Sophie."

Tyke shrugs. "That's what I told him, but he nearly ripped my head off when I mentioned that."

I take a deep breath and face forward. It's really crazy he doesn't expect me to move on. I don't get where he gets off thinking he should be able to have his cake and eat it too because news flash, this cake store is fucking closed.

We pull up to the club hosting the after party, and just like the last time I went to one of these, it's packed. Fans rush the SUV, and I tense, and kick myself for wishing for a split second Noel was with me. The bodyguard that's with us hops out and opens the door.

Tyke jumps out, practically right into the arms of a screaming group of female admires. A little nudge from Trip and I'm out and making my way inside. This place isn't quite as wild as the last. There are no half-naked women dancing in cages, but the dance floor over flows with bodies grinding to the beat. A couple men pass by me as I take in the surrounding and give me a suggestive look as they take in the sight of my short black skirt. I give them a polite smile, but turn away when they start their approach.

Trip and Tyke sit at a table signing autographs for what looks like a never-ending line of fans. I glance around and relax when I don't see any sign of Noel in the room. Hopefully he isn't coming.

I step up to the bar and order a beer. The skinny, blonde bartender doesn't bat an eyelash in my direction after multiple attempts at gaining her attention.

"Excuse me, love, but you look like you could use a drink." I turn to find Striker behind me with two beers in hand.

He winks at me as he hands me one of the beers, and I smile at him. He's looking good. Dark hair hangs loose around his face and the blue shirt he's wearing makes his eyes an impossibly deep brown.

I lick my lips and take a long draw from the beer.

Striker leans into me and places his hand on the small of my back. "You here alone?"

I nod. "If you're asking if I came with Noel, the answer's no."

He grins. "Brilliant! Care for a dance?"

I take another drink. This is what I came here to do—move on—and what better guy to do that with than this hunky specimen in front of me.

I take Striker's outstretched hand, and he curls his fingers around mine. He sets both of our bottles on the bar and tugs me towards the floor.

The minute we hit the floor, Striker pulls me in tight against his body. His hands roam down my back and then back up as he moves slowly against me. It's deliberate and sexy, like we are alone in a bedroom instead of a packed dance club. A tremor shoots through me as he slides a knee between mine. Deep brown eyes lock on mine as he threads his fingers into my hair.

My lips part, and my heart hammers. This feels really fast, but I'm willing to try it, if it gets rid of this hurt inside my chest. I pant as I close my eyes.

A sudden jerk startles me and my eyes snap open. Noel has Striker in a headlock, pulling him away from me. Striker shoots repeating elbows back into Noel's ribs, but he refuses to let go.

"You can't fucking take my girl!" Noel seethes. His eyes are boiling with rage.

My jaw drops. This is beyond ridiculous.

Within seconds, Mike and a few other bouncer-type men ascend upon the two tattooed rockers and yank them apart. Noel lunges for Striker while he's still locked in Mike's hold.

"Calm the fuck down!" Mike shouts at Noel.

He hauls him backwards toward the door. Noel's eyes refuse to leave me.

I roll my eyes. We need to seriously talk. He can't keep interfering with my life.

Striker straightens his shirt beside me, and it's the first time I notice all the curious stares by the other bar patrons. No doubt all of them are wondering what's so special about me to cause this fight between two rock stars.

He runs his fingers through his hair. "Blimey. That bloke has issues." Striker wraps an arm around my shoulders. "Where were we?"

I duck away from his arm and look at the door and watch Mike shove Noel unwillingly through it. The urge to confront him surges through me. We need to end this here and now, for good.

"I'm sorry, Striker. My ride is leaving without me. Maybe some other time?"

He frowns. "Your loss, love."

The little jab is enough to relieve any guilt I would've normally felt for leaving him stranded on the dance floor.

I rush through the club and out the door, just in time to catch up with Mike shutting Noel inside the Escalade. "Wait up! I'm going back with you."

Mike holds up his hands. "He's drunk. I don't think it's a good time for you to—"

I shake my head. "Now is the only time."

When I yank open the door, shock registers on Noel's face. "Lane? I knew you'd—"

I slam it once I'm inside. "Shut it, Noel. I didn't come here to make up. How could you do that to Striker? I'm trying to move on, damn it. This shit has to end."

The moment Mike shuts his door, the SUV starts for the bus.

Noel shakes his head. "No it doesn't. I love you."

I close my eyes and hold up my hand. "Stop. Stop saying stuff like that. It *does* have to end. How many times do I have to tell you, I won't be the other woman!"

He grabs my hand. "You're not."

I yank it away. "This ends, Noel. Tonight. Contract or not, I'm done."

"Lane…"

I turn away and stare out the window. "Please stop talking."

The rest of the ride back to Big Bertha, Noel doesn't say a word. The tension is thick and everyone, including the two men up front, can probably feel it.

The minute we park, I jump out of the vehicle and head for the bus. I'm over this. I'm over the tension and feeling trapped. If they sue me, what can they possibly get? I have nothing but a rented apartment. I don't even have a car, for crying out loud.

When I get back to the bedroom, I throw my suitcase on the bed. I yank a drawer open and throw my clothes in the bag. Tears threaten to spill from eyes. I know I'm throwing away everything, but I can't take being here one more minute. It just hurts too much.

"What are you doing?" Noel says from behind me.

A tear spills out of my eye, and I wipe it away with the back of my hand. "What's it look like I'm doing. I'm leaving."

"What about the contract?"

I shrug. "What about it? You can sue me if you want, but you aren't going to get much."

Noel's beside me, and he wraps his fingers around my wrist, successfully stopping me from packing. "I'm not going to sue you, Lane."

I face him as tears stream down my face. "Then why did you make me stay? I can't take this."

He pulls his lips into a tight line. "Using the contract against you was the only way I knew to make you stay. I don't want you to leave. I need you to stay with me."

"I can't, Noel. I can't let you hurt Sophie by being with me. If you commit to someone you should stand by it."

"But, I don't love her," he whispers. "I just want to be a good father."

I can see the need to prove that he's a better man than his dad in his eyes. Even if I love him, I'm not okay with him having a family with another girl and keeping me too.

"You'll be a great father. I know it. Irene will be thrilled to have a grandchild. You should really make up with your parents and figure out how to forgive Frank. All fathers make mistakes. Your first one was being with me."

Noel takes my hand. "I love you, Lane, so much. And you're right. That wasn't being the kind of father I want to be."

I hang my head. My heart tears at his words. I know he loves me, I can feel it in his words, but our timing is off. "Noel..."

He cups my face and forces me to look at him. "I hate this. The thought of losing you again—it tears me up. Tonight, when I walked in on Striker touching you, things went through my mind, and I nearly lost my fucking head. You're my heart, Lane. You're my everything."

A tear slips down my cheek. To know how much we hurt each other kills me. A sob escapes my lips. "I'm sorry, Noel. I never meant to hurt you."

His thumbs wipe the tears from my face. "I know, baby. It's not your fault. It's me who has to learn to let go. Don't blame yourself."

"I don't mean to hurt you."

He sighs and takes a stand of my hair between his fingers. "You can't worry about that. Losing you will hurt no matter what. Just promise me one thing."

I gaze into his eyes. "Anything."

"Promise that you don't hate me. I can't live with myself if you do."

I nod. "Yes. I promise."

Noel's lips crush down on me. I close my eyes and don't bother to fight what I know is our last kiss because he's not mine. Even though it's wrong, the sheer need to be with him, to please him in every way, vibrates through every cell in my body.

His hand knots into my hair, and I wrap my arms around his neck. My fingertips rub the skin on the back of Noel's neck. It's so warm and inviting under my touch. My heart pounds and suddenly I'm hot all over.

"I love you, Lane," Noel says against my lips. "Forever."

My breath leaves my chest and I feel a little dizzy.

He breaks our kiss and heat sears along my jaw as his lips work their way down my neck. I fist his shirt tight in my hands as I whimper. His large hand grips my thigh and hitches it around his hip as he slides his hand under my skirt. My legs open wider as his fingers trace the elastic edge of my panties. Once the fabric's aside, he teases my swollen folds with the tip of his finger.

I grab his hair and yank his mouth back to mine. Every inch of me aroused by his touch and I tear at his clothes. I want his skin on mine. I need to feel him.

Noel slides both hands up my side and peels my dress off. It lands in a heap by our feet as he directs his attention at exposing my breasts. One of his hands massages my breast while he bends down and wraps his lips around the other. I throw my head back and moan. It's amazing how he knows just what I like.

He yanks my panties down and then removes his own shirt and pants like he doesn't want to give me time to change my mind about this.

Our mouths meet, and he kisses me fiercely. With one swift move he has me down on the bed.

The mattress creaks with our weight, and Noel's eyes roam down my body. "You're so fucking beautiful."

I crush my lips to his, and the tip of him circles my moist flesh, each time hitting my clit and nearly making me lose my mind. I grind against him and he grins at my excitement. A trail of fire remains in the wake of his lips as they work their way down my shoulder. He works his hips in a slow steady motion, allowing the head of his cock to slide against my folds. Heat builds up in my core and after we connect once more, I explode.

Every inch of me clenches at the pure release of ecstasy.

Noel kisses me, and I moan into his mouth. His finds mine and circles it as he plunges himself inside me with one quick thrust. Fingernails on both of my hands rake down his back as he fills and stretches me in the most delightful ways.

"I love being inside you. It's my most favorite place on earth," he breaths against my lips.

I close my eyes and try to block out the thought that this will never happen again. That this is the last time I will feel this connection with Noel. I bite my lip as I pull my hips up to meet each thrust, allowing him to get deeper inside me.

Pretty soon, I feel the fire tugging at the pit of my belly again, and I know it won't be long until I come for the second time.

"God, Lane, I need you to let go with me. I don't want to be alone."

His words shove me over the edge, and I lose all control, at the same moment he grunts as he comes hard and fast inside me.

After he pulls himself out of me, he rolls over on his side and stares into my eyes. "I love you."

A tear streams down my face. "I love you, too. Forever."

We lay there in each other's arms, neither of us wanting to be the one to end the moment, but I know it can't last. I pull away from him, and he sits up.

He kisses the top of my head and then grabs a towel before heading to the shower. Once I hear the water turn on, I jump out of bed and quickly throw my clothes back on.

The suitcase I was packing got knocked on the floor when we were caught up in the moment. I bend down and stuff the clothes back in it, before I zip it up and make my way off the bus.

Chapter 25

The door on the bus slams shut, and I freeze. Damn. I was hoping to sneak out of here without being seen. I readjust the messy bun on the top of my head and attempt to smile as the footsteps boom up the steps. A gasp escapes me as my eyes land on the woman I saw on the internet, Sophie, with Noel's bodyguard, Mike. I fall back against the door, and the smile drops off my face. What the hell is she doing here? My eyes flit to my ragged appearance.

Shit.

Sophie is even more beautiful than her pictures. Her long, blonde hair sits in a high pony-tail, and her skin is flawless, nearly like porcelain. The baby bump she's sporting isn't very big, and really not that noticeable, unless you're looking for it, like me.

Being in the same room with this woman, who is about to give birth to Noel's child, twists my stomach into a huge knot. I take a deep breath and prepare myself for her to lash out.

She looks me up and down with blazing eyes. "Is this her?"

My heart leaps into my throat as the guilt of what I'd just done with Noel washes over me. I open my mouth to tell her I'm sorry, but no words come out. The shock of seeing her has me flabbergasted.

"Sophie, stop." Mike touches her arm.

Her face snaps towards him. "Don't you dare take her side!"

I swallow hard as Mike removes his hand and them throws them up in frustration. "You know what? I'm sick of this shit."

Her eyes narrow. "Shut up! Don't you say another word."

I glance between Mike and Sophie. Their exchange puzzles me. Mike has never gotten this personal with me, so why would he talk to her that way?

"What's going on out here?" Noel growls as he creeps up behind me.

I jump at the sound of his voice.

His eyes flit down to my bag. "You going somewhere?"

I bite my lip and shrug, not really wanting to have this argument in front of the mother of his soon-to-be-born child.

Sophie clears her throat and Noel turns toward her.

Her face goes from disdain into an angelic smile in less than a second. "Hey, baby."

My stomach turns, and tears threaten to spill from my eyes. That sweet term of endearment might as well be a knife straight into my heart.

She takes a couple steps towards him but halts instantly when he holds up a hand to stop her. "What are you doing here?"

She pokes her lip out. "I missed you."

Mike grunts beside her. "You're unbelievable!"

Her head whips toward him. "I said, shut up, Mike."

"No. I'm tired of this bullshit."

Noel crosses his arms over his chest, and furrows his brow. He's clearly confused about the tension between Mike and Sophie, too.

He steps closer. "Mike…? What the hell is going on, man?"

Mike sits down on the loveseat and frowns at me before he places his elbows on his knees. His tattooed arms strain as he drops his head into his hands and rubs the back of his buzzed head. "I fucked up."

I place a hand on Noel's forearm. The tension in the air tells me things are about to get ugly very fast.

Mike sighs. "Tell her, Soph. Tell them what we did."

Sophie snaps her head toward Mike. "Butt out, and learn to mind your own business."

He glares up at Sophie. "You don't think this is *my* fucking business? Either you tell them, or I will."

Her eyes widen. "I don't think I—"

"Damn it, Soph!" Mike shouts. "I can't live with this shit anymore. I can't stand lying to all of them. We're hurting people."

Laughter outside cuts through the silence on the bus—the rest of the guys are back from the club. Trip and Tyke make their way onto the bus with Riff in tow. The twins stop dead in their tracks. The tension in the small space is clear.

Riff clenches his jaw when he spots Sophie. Instantly, I feel for him because I know exactly how he feels after seeing the two of them together myself.

Trip clears his throat. "Should we leave? Looks serious in here."

Noel shakes his head as he glares at Mike and Sophie. "No. Stay. You're just in time to hear some secret Sophie's been keeping."

Trip pulls himself up on the counter, and Tyke leans next to him. Trip watches us like we are an entertaining movie—minus the popcorn—while Tyke pulls his lips into a tight line.

Riff flexes his jaw muscle and steps into Sophie's view. "How many more secrets can she possibly have?"

She doesn't even bother to acknowledge Riff as he stands beside Tyke.

Mike frowns at me, and my heart jumps into my throat. Whatever these two are hiding, it's bad, really bad. The agony is clear on Mike's face.

Sophie locks her gaze on me. I squeeze Noel's arm as I wait on her to speak.

She sighs. "The baby doesn't belong to Noel."

Noel's body tenses under my fingertips as he yells, "WHAT?" at the exact same time Riff does.

Mike stands beside Sophie and threads his fingers through hers. "It's mine."

Noel's hands fly into his hair, and he grabs handfuls of it in his fingers. He paces back and forth with his eyes closed.

He whips his head towards Riff, and a look of what seems like understanding passes between them.

"Told you I never fucked your girl," he says to Riff. "I would never do that shit to you!"

Riff's face twists in anger, and his nostrils flair. "You fucking slut!" he shouts before he storms off the bus.

A wave of nausea rolls through me. "Are you sure?"

Sophie nods. "I never slept with Noel."

I rub my forehead. Why the hell would she tell a lie like this? Why would Mike allow another man to claim his child? My heart shatters into a million pieces for Noel. His struggle to be a better man, the inner-war with himself, was all for a lie. There wasn't even a possibility that he was the father of her baby.

"How could you do this to me? You put me through pure fucking hell! Mike, man..." Noel growls in frustration. "I thought we were friends."

Mike doesn't answer, just drops his head again.

Noel glances up to the ceiling and lets out a sarcastic laugh. "I'm fucking out of here."

I grab his arm, but he flings me off and leaves without so much as another glance back. The bus door slams shut, and I jump a little inside my skin. Tyke pats his brother's shoulder and jerks a thumb towards the exit. The brothers stalk off after their friend.

I swallow hard when I realize everyone's left me alone with Mike and Sophie on the bus.

Sophie fidgets, clearly uncomfortable, drawing my attention to her. "What was the point in pinning your unborn baby on Noel when you and Mike are clearly together?"

She shrugs. "I didn't really have a choice at the time. The moment I found out I was pregnant, I panicked. Riff can't have children, and I knew that. Once he found out about Mike, he would have had Noel fire him. I love Mike, and I didn't want him to lose his job over being with me. That's why I did it. I knew if I blamed Noel, he wouldn't remember because he parties so damn much and sleeps with anything the moves—no offense—and Mike would be in the clear."

I twist my lips and stare at Mike. "I can't believe you went along with this. You're like his brother."

His shoulders slump, and he nods. "I know. That's what makes this so hard. It's been awful to watch him struggle. When you guys fought in the SUV last night, I saw first hand what this lie was doing to you both, and I felt guilty. All Noel ever talks about is being with you. How much he loves you. He says over and over that if it wasn't for the Sophie thing, the two of you could have it all. I had to make shit right, even if I lose my job. I love her, and I want to take care of *my* baby."

Tears burn my eyes. This entire time we could've been together. We've fought over someone else's lie. The weight of the damage done pushes down on me, and a sob escapes my lips. I bury my face in my hands. How can two people be so selfish? It's not okay to play with people's heads like that.

"Lanie…" Mike says, but I can't look at him.

I want to scream and yell at them. Tell them how evil they are. But I can't bring myself to do it. Sophie lied to try and protect someone that she loves, and I get that. It's not right and completely twisted, but I can respect it.

"I'm really sorry," Mike tries again.

I sniff and bat at the tears rolling down my cheek. "I think you all have done quite enough. You need to go."

Sophie's shoes click against the steps as Mike leads her down them. The door opens and then closes softly.

I glance down to my suitcase. Noel and the rest of the band are going to need some time to recover from this scandal. They don't need another girl hanging around and possibly coming between them.

I start towards the door and head for the group of Black Falcon roadies hanging out near the Escalades.

Hopefully, one of them will be nice enough to take me to the nearest airport.

Chapter 26

Nothing has changed in the two weeks I was away from Center Stage Marketing. All the employees work furiously on their computers as I pass by. Diana scheduled a meeting between us first thing this morning. I think she's anxious to see the plan I've come up with for Black Falcon's charity. I don't believe Noel ever told her I left the tour a few days early or else she would have just fired me over the phone.

The door to her office is open wide. I stick my head inside, and she waves me in. I take a seat across from her and balance my computer in my lap.

"Lanie, it's so good to see you, and congratulations for lasting the entire two weeks on tour. Noel called me this morning and said you stuck out your time like a champ. Not that it was a major task for you." She winks at me.

I swallow hard, feeling a little uncomfortable that she knows so much about my sex life. "Thank you, Ms. Swagger. I actually have the proposal done as well."

I flip open the screen and stand, but Diana holds up her hand. "No need for that, dear. The more experienced members of my team already outlined the project, and we have things in the works."

I tilt my head and furrow my brow. "You don't even want to see what I've come up with?"

She holds up her hand, like I'm being ridiculous. "You're only real job was to look pretty and keep Noel Falcon happy. And you've done just that. Leave the real work up to the rest of us."

I pull my lips into a tight line and slam the lid closed. "You were never going to take me seriously no matter what I did, were you?"

She pulls off her glasses. "Lanie, dear, the sooner you understand that certain people are used for their brains and others are meant to just look pretty, the better off you'll be. I'm a thinker—a visionary—while you're the type of person that can wrangle in the clients for me."

I blow a rush of air through my nose and roll my eyes. "Do you know how archaic that sounds? As a woman, surely you don't really think that way."

She shrugs. "That's reality, honey. You better get used to how things work here in the real world."

Anger boils through me. Part of me always knew she was using me, but I never imagined she would completely shut me down. She doesn't even want to give my work a chance. Suddenly, the dream of working under her doesn't seem like such a grand idea anymore.

I lift my chin. "You know what, Diana, I quit."

She flinches. "You can't quit. Have you forgotten about the contract you signed with me?"

"I didn't forget. I made it my two weeks on tour, so you can't sue me, and there's nothing you can do if I quit now."

He eyes narrow. "You'll never get another job in this town again."

I shrug. "The non-compete was only for New York. I'm fine with leaving this state if this is how business is done here."

Her jaw drops. No one is going to treat me like a piece of meat, especially not her. The expression on her face shows, that never in a million years did she expect an intern like me, to tell her that she can basically shove her job up her ass. I grin at that thought and turn around, without a second of hesitation, and walk out.

****

"I can't believe you quit!" Aubrey says as she watches me pack my suitcase.

I smile as I think about the smug look on Diana's face disappearing when I quit. "Believe it. That woman's a tyrant."

She pokes out her bottom lip. "You sure you can't stay here? There are a thousand other jobs in this city other than marketing."

I zip up my suitcase. "I love marketing. That's where my heart lies. It sucks that I can't stay here with you, but going back home will be good. Mom misses me like crazy, and I can find a job in Houston or something." I set my bag on the floor and pull up the handle until it clicks. "I think I'm all set."

Aubrey steps around the bed and wraps her arms around my neck. I close my eyes and lean into her as a tear escapes down my cheek. I hate leaving her. She's the only thing I don't want to leave behind. She rubs big circles on my back. "It's going to be okay, sweetie. You and Noel can finally have your happily ever after."

I squeeze her tight. "I don't know if we can. The entire time we've been fighting over him having a girl pregnant, he asked me not to leave him—to let him show me I wasn't second to him. Then at the first sign of a problem in our relationship, I ran. I don't know if he'll forgive me for walking away from him a second time."

She pats my head. "Sure he will. True love can get through anything. He'll forgive you."

God, how do I even go about fixing this? The whole thing is one big clusterfuck.

She pulls back and wipes her eyes. "Go on, before I decide to hold you hostage here."

I frown. "You sure you're going to be alright by yourself?"

She sniffs and then smiles. "Are you kidding? Now I can have all the wild sex parties I want with you gone. Maybe I can even get Riff to visit."

I roll my eyes. "I'll tell him you miss his…"

She smacks my arm. "Don't you dare tell him that, no matter how true it is. That boy has one giant—"

I shove my fingers in my ears. "La! La! La! La! Not listening to you!"

She laughs. "Go on smartass, before you miss your flight. Riff says the pass to get into the V.I.P show for tonight will be at the door under 'Long-Dick Dong'?"

I shake my head. "Those guys really love giving that pseudo name. I'm so glad to hear he and Noel are working things out since Mike finally told them the truth."

She sighs. "Me too. I can't believe that bitch would do that to them. Doesn't she know she nearly destroyed one of the greatest rock bands ever?"

"Love makes people do insane things, Aubrey. Look at me. I'm traveling cross country to apologize to a man I'm not even sure wants me anymore. He's not called once in the last couple days since he learned the truth. This is probably a mistake."

She pushes my long hair over my shoulder. "The only mistake when it comes to love, is not going for it."

****

I practice everything I want to say in the cab as we speed towards the venue of tonight's show. Black Falcon is doing a small acoustic show to kick off the children's literacy campaign for a small audience of three hundred people. I read on the internet the ticket prices jumped up to nearly three hundred a piece for a person to attend such an intimate event.

Aubrey arranged for Riff to leave me a ticket at the entrance after she advised him not to tell Noel I'm coming. I don't want to cause a scene before the show, so I figure I'll slip backstage and talk with him after.

The cab driver stops at the entrance of the A&R Bar and I slide some cash to him before I slip out the door. My heart thunders in my chest as I walk through the entrance. This is it. He's somewhere in this building.

I collect my pass from the girl at the door after she snickers at the ridiculous name Riff left it under. Someday I'm going to have to speak with these guys about changing their incognito name.

A small stage sits along the far-back wall, and tables and chairs are arranged to face it. Every seat is packed, except for one in the left corner furthest back from the stage. Silently, I say a prayer of thanks. The further back I sit the better. I don't want to distract Noel. These people paid a ton of money to watch him sing for an hour.

Chatter all around me dies down as soon as the guys take the stage. Their normal grand entrances aren't anywhere insight. Instead the guys smile and wave as they take their seats to play an all acoustic set. My eyes lock on Noel as he sets a bottle of water on the floor beside him. The distressed jeans and black t-shirt he's wearing hug his body perfectly. Dark hair sticks up in every direction and has that messy look that I find unbelievably sexy. Even from a distance, I can see he looks beat down and tired, not his usual upbeat cocky self. A pain in my chest hits me hard and I clutch my shirt in my hand.

He pulls the mic up to his lips and says a simple, "Hello."

Trip starts off the beat, thumping rhythmically on a box looking thing, while Tyke and Riff strum their guitars. Noel nods his head and closes his eyes as he sings. His voice is always beautiful, but this time it sounds different. A little more tortured.

Every song goes on that way, most of the time his eyes remaining shut as he belts out the words. Finally, he announces to the crowd this was their last song, and I know it's almost time to face him. When the last chorus break happens, I stand and grab my suitcase to find my way closer to the stage. As I near the security team, I flash them the backstage pass Riff left for me.

"Lane?" Noel's voice echoes around the room. "Is that really you?"

This is exactly what I wanted to avoid—a public scene—but I know I have no choice now. I turn slowly, and our eyes lock. His lips quirk up before he bends down to whisper in Riff's ear. He stands and meets my stare again. Riff nods and leans over toward Trip and Tyke to fill them in on whatever Noel just told him.

He brings the mic up to his lips. "This song goes out to the girl who is my everything. I'm not an easy man to love, and music is about the best way I know how to express my feelings to her. This is called *Faithfully*."

Riff plays out a few notes on his guitar, and I instantly recognize the melody made famous by *Journey*.

After the song intro, Noel's voice blends into the acoustic chords beautifully. He takes a couple slow steps before hopping off the stage. His eyes fixate on me while coming closer with each step he takes. My heart pounds as he stops directly in front of me. He sings the sweet words about life on the road being tough and how loving a man involved in the music business is hard. Especially, when things don't always go the way they're supposed, too. Noel's eyebrows pull in as he gazes into my eyes and continues the verse. The last few lines he directs to me. They are about me standing by him through everything and that he's mine, *forever*, and faithfully.

A lump catches in my throat and I swallow hard, trying not to cry in front of a room full of strangers.

Noel grabs my hand and threads his fingers through mine. I squeeze his hand as a tear slips down my cheek. He lets my hand go and brushes it away with his thumb while he continues to sing. He says he's lost without me, and being apart isn't easy, but we need to learn to fall in love all over again.

He sings, *"Faithfully. Oh oh oh oh…"*

A sob escapes me, and everything I planned on saying to him flies out the window. I can feel how much he loves me through the passion in these lyrics. Noel drops the microphone on the ground, and a loud thud snaps around the room. He cups my face and pulls it to his. Tears stream down both our faces, and he leans in and presses his lips to mine.

"Forever," he whispers. "I'm yours."

ACKNOWLEDGEMENTS

I know it's been said many times that it takes a village to create a book, but I still have to say it. This novel would not have seen the light of day if it wasn't for the talented eyes of some pretty amazing people. GGBT members, Emily Snow, Katie Ashley, and Kelli Maine, you three rock my world so much. Over the years, we've become awesome friends, and I am so thankful for that. I owe everything I've learned about writing and the biz to you guys. I have some serious love for you all!

My early readers, Jennifer Wood, Rachael Allen, Melanie Kramer-Santiago, Tanya Keetch, Marilyn Medina, Pen your keen eyes caught a ton of things in this manuscript in those early reads. Thank you so much for all the time you put into it and embracing me into the romance community! I've met so many awesome people there, and I can't thank them enough for all the love and support they've shown me. I truly love you guys bunches!

Of course, I have to give props to the world of rock. Without awesome music, the world would be lifeless.

Last, but not least, big thanks to my darling husband and son. I would be nothing without you two. Love you, always.

And a huge thanks to my readers. You all rock so much!

9-14

DISCARD

15264613R00185

Made in the USA
San Bernardino, CA
20 September 2014